THE LONESOME
AUTOCRAT

THE LONESOME AUTOCRAT

By Alice Zogg

Aventine Press

This book is a work of fiction.

Published by Aventine Press
1023 4th Ave #204
San Diego CA, 92101
www.aventinepress.com

ISBN: 1-59330-420-X

Library of Congress Control Number: 2006932491
Library of Congress Cataloging-in-Publication Data
The Lonesome Autocrat/Alice Zogg
Printed in the United States of America

To Leo and Annelore

CREDITS

Many thanks are in order to Walter Fehlmann for familiarizing me with his model-train hobby. Credit is due to my sister-in-law, Annelore, for sharing her knowledge of the Davos, Switzerland locale. Again, Valoise Douglas did an excellent job of editing. I appreciate your good eye for detail, Val! My daughter, Franziska, came to the rescue with her expertise about the ins-and-outs of court reporting. She also applied herself once more to the prosaic job of proofreading another of my mystery tales. Last, but not least, I thank Pat Yankosky for her superb artwork for the book cover design.

CAST OF CHARACTERS:

R.A. Huber Private detective and narrator of this story

Peter Huber R.A. Huber's husband; an amateur writer

Otto Sonderegger Ruler of Talblick; made his fortune in the hotel industry

Erika Graff Otto's daughter; Huber's childhood friend

Alex Sonderegger Otto's son; a banker

Mirella Sonderegger Alex's wife; shows a bit of a Latin temper

Lotti Sonderegger Teenage daughter of Alex and Mirella; is bored at Talblick

Norbert Sonderegger Otto's son; an antiques dealer

Karl Sonderegger Otto's youngest son from a second marriage; the black sheep of the family

Helga Hodler Long-time housekeeper at Talblick; has been taking care of the household for some 50 years

Laura Thompson	Court reporter from the USA; hired by Otto Sonderegger to transcribe his memoirs
Fritz Moritz	Otto's old chum; often comes for a visit
Claude Boreau	Erika's boyfriend; prefers to converse in French
Rita Schmied	Cleaning lady; likes to gossip
Hans Weber	Otto's masseur; keeps his opinions to himself
Rex	Otto's German shepherd; a dog in harmony with his master
Ernst Knupp	Detective of the Kantonspolizei Graubünden, Kriminal Abteilung; in charge of case

Chapter 1

The train roared into Davos station before eleven on a Wednesday morning in August. I grabbed my upright suitcase, stepped off, and walked the short distance to the taxi stand. I spotted an empty cab and hopped in.

"Where to?" asked the driver.

"Hotel Sondereggli, please."

Moments later, he dropped me off in front of the familiar place. I checked in, unpacked, and then called my childhood friend, Erika Graff.

"Hi, Erika! It's Regula."

"Well, hello! What a pleasant surprise! When are you coming to Europe?"

"I'm already here, in Switzerland, to be exact," I replied.

"Well, I'll be darned. So you're in Zurich already?"

"Actually, I'm in Davos."

"What?" she exclaimed excitedly. "So how come you and Peter didn't just drive up to our house? Didn't you rent a car?"

I replied, "Peter and I separated and - -"

She interrupted, "Sorry to hear that."

"You misunderstand. We are getting along just fine. What I mean is, Peter and I parted in Zurich and are traveling in different directions. He took the rental car to Geneva where he'll attend a literary convention, and he also plans to visit several of his friends in that region. I'm traveling by train and look forward to reuniting with some of mine. You're first!"

"Gotcha! Give me about twenty-five minutes and I'll pick you up at the station."

"I've already checked in at your father's hotel."

"At the Sondereggli? Why did you do that?"

Mockingly I asked, "Isn't it a good hotel?"

"Of course it's good, even though Papa doesn't own it any longer. But why not simply stay with us at Talblick?"

"I don't want to impose on you."

"Don't be silly. We'll discuss your lodgings later. See you soon," and she hung up.

Chapter 2

While waiting for my friend in the hotel lobby, I was dwelling in the past. Erika's parents had been good friends with my folks. When we were kids, I had spent numerous summer vacations as well as the annual week of the winter sports school-break at Talblick, the Sonderegger residence. Erika and I were close in age and great pals. We kept in contact after my move to the United States. I always made a point to see her when on trips in Europe, and she had visited me in California a few times over the years.

I mused about my friend's encounter with devastating tragedy, having lost her husband and son all at once. The two men had fallen to their deaths in a mountain climbing accident. Widowed at the age of forty-six, she had moved back in with her father and now, fourteen years later, she still lived with him.

I was just wondering how life was treating her up on the hill at Talblick, when she came toward me with outstretched arms, exclaiming, "Regula, my old friend! Terrific to see you!"

As we embraced in European fashion, hugging cheeks, - - left, right, left - - I said, "It's sure good to be here."

Then I stepped back and surveyed her at arms' length. Her wavy auburn hair was pulled back at the sides and ended about an inch above the shoulders in a casual do. A pair of intelligent gray eyes peered at me below straight brows. The shape of her eyebrows had always fascinated me. She was approximately 5'8", about two inches taller and 20 pounds heavier than me. I remembered that she used to be painfully thin.

I remarked, "You look great, Erika! You've filled out a little, and it's becoming."

"Thanks," she replied, "and you're in as great a shape as ever!" Then she said, "All right, are you ready to come up to the house?"

"Let me invite you for lunch first, so we can catch up on what's going on in our lives," I answered.

"Fair enough."

The hotel restaurant was not busy, the lunch crowd not having arrived yet. We were seated at a window table and ordered *Bündnerfleisch*, a specialty of the region, which is a particular type of dried beef. It had been many years since I last tasted that palatable dish, so I savored every bite.

After the meal, sipping our coffee, Erika said, "Conversing via e-mail is good, but nothing beats talking to you face to face." She continued, "I admire you for having the guts to be in the sleuthing business. What do you call it?"

"Simply R.A. Huber," I answered.

"How is it coming along?"

"I can't complain; I've been busy lately."

"Have you solved many murder cases?"

"A few."

"Tell me about them."

I stated, "I don't like to discuss my cases. Besides, I'm on vacation!"

"Have it your way," she shrugged. Then she smiled and said, "I've read one of Peter's books. I was so engrossed that I couldn't put it down. I read the entire work in two days! He's immensely talented."

"I agree," I said proudly.

"So tell me all about your trip. Where have you been so far?"

I replied, "We flew into Zurich and spent a couple of days with my sister. Then we rented a car and drove to the South Tyrol. We stayed in Merano for two days. The town appeared more Austrian than Italian."

Erika put in, "I've never been to Merano. I've heard it is beautiful."

I nodded. "It's a picturesque little place surrounded by mountains. Of course, Italian and German are spoken there. We took this funny-looking one-person chairlift at the base of the town going up a mountain. Once we got to the summit, we felt on top of the world! We even found a hotel and restaurant at the peak. Then we traveled on, over the Reschen Pass, came down the other side and cruised along the absolutely gorgeous Reschen See area. To our surprise the border between Italy and Austria doesn't exist anymore. Driving through the Arlberg tunnel, I got claustrophobic. I thought we'd never see daylight again! I was getting close to panic for the last few kilometers, holding the steering wheel so tight it hurt."

She teased, "And I always thought you were fearless!"

I continued, "We spent one night in Feldkirch, Austria. The old town district is worth exploring."

"Yes, I've been to Feldkirch. Where did you go from there?"

By now I felt comfortable in my role as tour-guide and went on, "We made our way back to Switzerland and headed for *"la Suisse romande"* via Vaduz in Liechtenstein, Walenstadt, Zurich, Bern, Lausanne and spent the night in Morges before we crossed over to France."

My friend put in, "What a long drive in one day going from one end of Switzerland to the other!"

"It wasn't too bad and mostly freeway driving," I shrugged. "Up until then, the weather was nice. Once in France, we had nothing but rain and cool temperatures. Aix-les-Bains would have been a charming town sporting a beautiful harbor, but the heavy rains spoiled it for us. We traveled to Annecy hoping for a better climate, but again were out of luck. We bought umbrellas and managed to explore the charming 'Vieil Annecy' on foot. The town paints a fairy tale picture with its old-fashioned vibrantly colored houses, canals, little bridges and passages, shops and outdoor cafes. All of old town is strictly reserved for pedestrians; no cars allowed."

She remarked, "That storm hit here too. It rained for a week and we only saw sunshine again three days ago."

"I know. When we crossed back into Switzerland and decided to spend a couple of days in Rapperswil, it was raining cats and dogs! From there we headed back to Zurich where Peter and I parted company."

Then, grinning, I said, "Now I'm here and all yours!"

"Good! How long can you stay?"

"I'm playing it by ear. The hotel reservation is for two nights, but they assured me that if I decided to stay longer there would be no problem to accommodate me. I have friends in Bad Ragaz and might pay them a visit while in this part of the country."

"We'll talk about your accommodations later." And she urged, "You must stay a few days. The *Chilbi* is going to be in town this coming weekend."

Delighted, I inquired, "So you still have the carnival coming to your village?"

"Every year around this time."

After a pause, I said, "Now Erika, tell me all about your life."

"There isn't much to tell. I still work out of my home as a computer programmer."

"Do you like the job?"

"Sometimes. And other times I hate it."

"How is your father?"

"In remarkably good health for a man of eighty-four," she replied.

"Is he still showing a forceful personality, or has he mellowed with age?"

"Delicately put, Regula!" And she continued, "No, age has not made him docile. He is the same tyrant as always. I think he's even getting worse."

"And how are your brothers?"

"If you stick around long enough you can see for yourself. They've all been summoned by Papa."

"What's the occasion?"

"No special occasion," she said. "Papa tends to order the entire family to gather at Talblick at least once a year for no other reason than to taunt everyone, it seems."

"Really?"

"Papa has never forgiven the boys for their lack of interest in taking over the hotel business. The Sonderegger dynasty has come to an end, which has enraged him for years."

"I can understand his feelings," I said.

"Sure, but it's not the end of the world!"

I looked around the restaurant and saw that the place had filled up. There wasn't an empty table in sight. After motioning to the waiter for the bill, I turned to my childhood pal and suggested, "Let's move on and give some other folks a chance to eat."

Chapter 3

As Erika drove through Davos, one of Europe's oldest mountain resorts, I exclaimed, "Wow! The town has gotten huge! I'm amazed at the amount of hotels, restaurants and clubs!"

"Yes, it has expanded. During the meeting of the World Economic Forum held here every January, all these locales are packed to capacity."

I remarked, "I'm aware that Davos is one of the most popular resorts in Switzerland, but I wasn't prepared for its size."

She said proudly, "Summer or winter, we have a lot to offer. There are health spas, a sports center, museums, as well as concert halls and theaters. Whether you're interested in hiking, mountain biking, downhill or cross-country skiing, snowboarding, hang gliding, golfing, tennis, or if you are an ice hockey fan, it's all here for you."

As we got to the outskirts of Davos Platz, I gazed at the mountain range to our left and asked, "Is that the *Pischa* ski area?"

"No," she corrected, "*Pischa* is behind us. You're pointing at *Jakobshorn*."

Soon after we had passed Davos, the village -- simply called Dörfli -- came into view. Dörfli, like Davos, is located at the foot of the mountain valley.

When we drove along the main street of the village, I observed, "Dörfli appears to have grown too." And pointing east toward the base of the mountains, I added, "Looks like a settlement of new houses over there."

She nodded, saying, "They've been popping up in the last few years."

At the end of the village we turned left and climbed the steep and curvy road leading up to Talblick.

I said, "I forgot that the road is so narrow. I doubt there is enough room for another car to get by. What do you do when one approaches from the opposite direction?"

She replied, "Oh, we manage. We have to be alert on this road, though. If a car coming from the other direction is not visible, at least the motor can be heard. Then we wait at a slightly wider part of the road for the other vehicle to pass by. In worst case, a car has to be backed into one of the few turnouts along the way. Some people unfamiliar with this road honk their horn at every curve. And remember, this street leads to Talblick only, so there isn't much traffic."

"Well, I'm glad you're the driver!"

Soon we had turned around the last bend and arrived at the plateau where the estate came into view. Apart from the impressive size, there was nothing architecturally remarkable about the mansion sitting on top of the hill. The building was cube-shaped with simple, uncluttered lines, a flat roof, and long, cantilevered sun terraces.

I commented, "The house looks pretty much the way I remember it."

"From the outside, perhaps, but the interior has been modernized many times over the years. There are lots more bathrooms now."

She let me out and proceeded to park the car in the attached garage at the side of the house. I stood and surveyed the panorama below. The view stretched from Dörfli, directly beneath, over the entire Davos area with the Davoser See at the end, and to the mountain range beyond. No wonder the residence was named *Talblick*, which translates to "Valley View."

When Erika joined me, I marveled, "I'd forgotten what a glorious view you have into the valley!"

"On a clear day like today, one can see far," she agreed. Then she asked, "Do you want to go inside and say hi to Papa, or do you prefer to walk around the grounds first?"

"Are there any horses galloping around?"

She giggled and stated, "You're safe, Regula! We don't keep horses anymore."

"I'm sorry to hear that for your dad's sake." Then I said, "I would love to take a stroll around."

We went along the side of the mansion to the backyard. We passed the large veranda stretching alongside the dining and living room. It was decked out with patio furniture and a few yards farther, a hammock hung tied between two trees.

"Must be relaxing, lounging in that," I remarked.

"I like to sit in it and read, whenever I find myself with leisure time," she said.

We came upon the clay tennis court, and I inquired, "Is it still played on?"

"Rarely. Papa had to give up playing, and I sort of lost interest too."

"It appears in good condition. What a shame it's not being used."

"Oh, Papa keeps it up. He still sponsors a tournament every spring."

We strolled on, and when I saw the horse stables, I asked, "So these are empty?"

She assured me, "There are no more horses in there. The stables were converted into additional garage space."

"I can imagine your father misses his equine charges."

"Of course he does, even though he won't admit it."

We made our way back to the house, and when we reached the patio, a robust, gray-haired woman opened the sliding-glass door, saying, "Here you are. I thought I heard you drive into the garage earlier."

As our eyes made contact, I asked, "Helga?"

"Yes?"

I exclaimed, "How wonderful to still find you at Talblick!"

She gave me a puzzled look.

"You don't remember me? I'm Regula."

She blurted, "Of course! Little Regula! You looked familiar, but I couldn't place you."

Erika asked her, "Where is Papa?"

"I think he's in the train room," the housekeeper replied.

Then my friend turned to me and said, "Do you mind if I finish some work I started? It won't take long."

"Of course not. Go ahead."

"Helga will take you to see Papa. I'll join you shortly," and she quickly stepped inside.

Helga smiled and said, "This way, please." As I followed the old housekeeper through the sliding-glass door, she asked, "What do I call you now?"

"Regula, as always," I replied.

Keeping in step with her through the living room and then down the long corridor, I inquired, "What's a train room?"

"Mr. Sonderegger plays with toy trains."

How bizarre, I thought.

Chapter 4

A German shepherd was sprawled in front of the door. At our approach the dog sharpened his ears, got to his feet and let out a couple of barks.

Helga commanded, "*Platz*, Rex!" and the dog moved aside and obediently sat on his hind legs. She opened the door and said, "Go ahead. Rex is not allowed in the room," and left.

I'm not sure what I expected to find in the train room, but what I discovered when entering was beyond my wildest imagination. The gigantic room consisted of what I took for a miniature replica of the Swiss railroad system. The trains were running in perfect synchrony amid an intriguing network of stations, tunnels, bridges and mountain passes. At street intersections the crossing gates were automatically lowered seconds before trains rushed by, and raised again when they had passed.

Over this train paradise, standing in an elevated mobile cart similar to the kind of cherry picker used by electricians and tree trimmers, was Otto Sonderegger. He conducted the complex system with what looked like a mini-computer, about the size of a calculator. The position from above gave him a sort of aerial overview. Along the walls there was enough space for people to walk on the outside of the display, but the impressive exhibit took up the entire center of the room.

I watched, fascinated, for some minutes. The typically Swiss locomotives with their overhead wires were pulling passenger as well as freight trains. I also spotted a couple of double-deckers, and winding up a curvy mountain pass was a steam engine with actual smoke coming out of its stack.

Entire towns and villages were displayed, with churches, schoolhouses, cars, bicycles, people, pets and all. There were farms surrounded by open fields where cows and horses grazed, as well as forests with deer nestling in a clearing.

The old man looked down at me from his throne and said, "Hi there, Regula! How do you like my trains?"

"Hello Mr. Sonderegger. They are fabulous! What an absolutely intriguing hobby you've gotten involved in!"

"I'm gratified with how this room has turned out," he stated. Then he pushed a lever and mechanically maneuvered his bucket sideways, then lowered it until it came to rest beside me. As he stepped out of it I got a chance to survey him up close. He still stood tall and erect but now had a full head of white hair. The clean-shaven face showed aging, no doubt, but it was still a strong face. The determined look in the gray eyes and the stubbornly pointed chin remained.

I asked, "May I have a closer look?"

"I give you permission! Take your time," he replied mockingly.

I made my way along the walls, stopping here and there to examine the site in detail. There was a tramway with red cabins going up and down a mountain cliff, and on another peak with permanent snow, I observed a chairlift and little figures of skiers scattered on the slopes. The St. Gotthard scenery including the village of Wassen particularly intrigued me. The famous Church of Wassen appeared to be an exact replica of the real thing. A train was just about to enter the St. Gotthard tunnel with its piggyback load of trucks. I gazed in awe at a spectacular lake scene close to the outer edge of the display. The miniature lake looked authentic, with sailboats anchored at one shore and a formidable waterfall rushing into it at another.

I noticed a shelf on the wall near the window neatly arranged with tools; screwdrivers, pliers, a drill with several sizes of drill bits, a hammer and nails, glue and more. So I asked, "Did you build all this yourself?"

"Most of it, but I bought a lot of stuff already finished. The locomotives, wagons, tracks and buildings I purchased. Some of the merchandise was ready to be installed, and others had to be assembled."

"But you built the basics from scratch?"

"Of course."

"How did you go about doing that? I mean, give me a rough idea. I have no clue of where one would begin with creating such a magnificent site."

He chuckled and said, "You haven't changed. You were always a curious kid, as I recall."

Then he explained, "I started out with lots of plywood to construct the basic layout, and then I nailed or glued the tracks onto the structure. Next I built all the tunnels, bridges and overpasses, using papier-mâché to create mountains, landscaping, et cetera. I constructed the shapes with chicken wire and then papier-mâchéd over and around it. Once everything was installed and dry, I was ready to paint the terrain. Little by little, I added the towns, villages and so forth."

"How did you make the trees and bushes?"

"The pine trees for the forest, I purchased. The others I created out of bendable plastic skeletons and then formed the branches into shape and glued on ground foam for foliage."

Then I pointed to a section covered with plastic sheeting close to the miniature lake and asked, "What's under there?"

"That's the newest project I'm working on. I'm rather proud of it. I should have it completed in the next few days, and then I'll unveil the area and show it off."

I remarked, "Installing the cart so you can conduct the entire show from above is clever!"

He replied, "I can run the trains standing on the floor; I need the bucket-lift when building scenes in spots not accessible from the sides. I was replacing a light bulb that had gone out in one of the houses. That's why I was in the cart just now."

"Oh, are the buildings lighted? I hadn't noticed."

He went over to the large window and pulled the heavy floor-to-ceiling curtains closed. As darkness settled over the train paradise, we saw lights glowing from inside the mini-buildings, houses and churches. The streetlights in the miniature towns also came to life. The trains moving along on the tracks, going in and out of tunnels with only their headlights showing, gave the display a ghost-like image.

"Wow!" I exclaimed, "what a spectacular night-show!"

Mr. Sonderegger drew the curtains back to let the sunlight in again. Then he pushed a button on his controls, and suddenly everything came to a halt. The roar of trains moving rapidly along the rails had ceased. The only sound left came from the steady rush of the waterfall built into the miniature mountainside flowing to the lake.

He said, "I'm thirsty. I don't allow food or drink in this room. There is nowhere to sit anyway. Let's go to the veranda."

He led the way out of his train wonderland. The dog, waiting by the door, wagged his tail at the sight of his master.

Mr. Sonderegger said, "Come, Rex," and the canine jumped to his feet and kept up with the long strides of his owner. As I followed them down the hallway, I marveled at the old gentleman's powerful physique. Incredible that this man is eighty-four years old, I thought.

Chapter 5

We were sitting on comfortable patio chairs on the veranda, sipping iced tea. Rex had been ordered to stay put on the lawn nearby.

I remarked, "I'm surprised you recognized me right away."

My host replied, "I was forewarned! Erika told me you called and that she was bringing you here. Besides, you haven't changed much since I saw you last at your father's funeral."

I nodded.

Then he asked, "What's this I hear about you staying at the Sondereggli? That won't do."

"I don't want to be a burden."

"Nonsense. You're staying with us."

I protested, "I understand you're going to have all your family here soon, and another extra person might be too much of an imposition."

"You know perfectly well that we have plenty of room at Talblick for any extra people I wish to invite."

Smiling, I said, "I was mainly thinking of Helga. I don't want to add more work for her."

"Helga is as healthy and capable as ever. If she needs help in the kitchen, Erika can lend a hand." And he said commandingly, "So that's settled. I'm going to call the Sondereggli people and have them bring up your luggage."

"I've already unpacked my things, and I made a reservation for two nights."

"All right. So spend tonight in Davos, but starting tomorrow you'll stay with us."

He reached into his back trouser pocket for his cell phone, and before I could prevent it, he made the call canceling my second night's reservation at the hotel. Apparently they hadn't argued with him.

I asked, "Did you sell all of your hotels, or just the Sondereggli?"

"The whole caboodle, and it's all in strangers' hands now."

I realized I had touched a sore spot. I had no wish to let him air his contempt about the lack of interest his sons had shown for taking over the business.

So I went on, "I always thought you used your last name in a clever way by dubbing your hotel *Sondereggli*, 'Special Little Corner'."

"The credit goes to my late father who thought that up," he replied.

"Oh, I didn't realize that the hotel business was already in your family a generation before. I was under the impression that you had started it all."

"My father owned the Sondereggli, which I took over after his death. Then, over the years, I added more hotels."

"I see."

He continued, "Mind you, the business wasn't always prosperous. We had plenty of hardships."

"Oh?"

"I was born into it, if you will. Instead of playing soccer with the other boys, I would come straight from school and pitch in at the hotel."

"What were your duties?"

"Mostly helping the porter, but during high-season if we were short-handed, I was put to work where needed. We had no elevators in those days. Hauling luggage up four flights of stairs was strenuous work for a boy of twelve or thirteen, but I didn't mind. I enjoyed chatting with the guests, finding out where they were from and what they planned to do on their vacation. The tips came in handy too."

I inquired, "Did you have any siblings?"

"Two older sisters, but by that time they were married and long gone." And, grinning, he went on, "I was either born by accident, or my parents added me as an afterthought!"

Then he continued, "Shortly after I came back from the hotel management school, war broke out."

"World War II?"

"Of course. Was there any other?" And he reminisced further, "During the war everyone in the country fell on bad times. The hotel industry was hit especially hard. The borders were closed off, so foreign tourism came to a halt for six years. We had to solely depend on the small amount of Swiss folks who could still afford vacations. Father had to let most of his hotel staff go, but somehow we struggled through the war years and kept the Sondereggli going."

"By 'we,' how many people are you talking about?"

"You can count them on one hand. Father, Mother, a chambermaid and myself, if you disregard my absences while on active duty."

"I'm impressed! By active duty, do you mean the military?"

"Of course."

"I don't understand. Switzerland was not at war."

He stated, "We had to be ready for a possible invasion nonetheless. Being neutral was no guarantee. The little man with the funny mustache could have decided to march through our country rather than go around it."

"I hadn't thought of that," I said.

After a pause, he continued, "I took the hotel over at the age of twenty-five. The struggle and worry during the war years had left their mark on Father and he died soon afterwards."

I commented, "By that time you were married and Erika was a baby."

"Correct."

Then I asked, "Did you also inherit Talblick?"

"No. I had Talblick built a few years later, as I got more prosperous. Early on, we used the house as a bed-and-breakfast."

"Now I understand why there's always been so many extra rooms."

We sat in silence for some time, and then he asked, "Where is Erika, anyhow?"

"She thought you would entertain me while she finished some work." And chuckling I added, "Are you tired of me already, Mr. Sonderegger?"

"Not yet," he grunted.

Then he abruptly got to his feet and ordered, "Let's go for a walk."

Chapter 6

We had passed the stables, now converted into garages, and were walking through a pasture. I was wearing sandals with a two-inch heel and was almost running, trying to keep up with the old man. For each of his steps, I had to take two. Rex, trotting along happily at the other side of his master, had no trouble keeping the pace.

Pointing at the dog, I asked, "You never put him on a leash?"

"Certainly not on my own property!"

At the end of the field the old horse trail was still intact, and Mr. Sonderegger guided us along the track.

"When did you give up your horses?"

"Two years ago," he replied.

"You must have had a good reason?"

"It wasn't my reasoning, but the doctor insisted. He had suggested I give up sports if I didn't want to be a candidate for a hip replacement. So I stopped playing tennis. I didn't consider riding a sport; after all, the horse does all the work. One day I twisted my body while in the saddle, and the result was that I could barely walk for months. So there was no sense in keeping the horses once I couldn't ride any longer. Erika had lost interest in the activity a long time before that happened."

"I'm sorry to hear this."

"Well, it saves me the expense of stable help," he commented.

His attempt at humor did not fool me. I could tell he missed his horses passionately.

I asked, "How is your hip now?"

"Better," he replied. "I had extensive physical therapy and my masseur still gives me daily massages."

Then he said, "Are you disappointed about the horses? Were you planning on riding?"

"Good grief, no! I only made one attempt at riding, and I got kicked before I even had the chance to mount the horse. The incident scared me to death and I've kept my distance from horses ever since."

"What happened?"

"The mishap occurred here at Talblick when I was about eleven."

"Really? I don't recall." And after a pause he exclaimed, "Wait a minute, I think I remember now. The girl in the tree, was that you?"

I nodded.

He burst out laughing and said, "That was hilarious!"

"I didn't think it was funny at the time, and I had a hole in my thigh for years."

Still amused, he reminisced, "I came to see what all the commotion was about, and there you were, sitting up in a tree. When I ordered you to come down, you told me, 'No, sir.' So you stubbornly stayed in that tree until all the horses had returned to the stables." And he continued, "You seemed an obstinate little girl. I haven't come across many people who say 'no' to me."

Then he said, "I can't remember. What did you do to the horse to get kicked in the first place?"

"I didn't know any better and approached the animal from the back."

"Stupid of you! You deserved to be kicked."

During the entire time we had this conversation, he had not slowed his pace for a second. The terrain had led steadily uphill for some time, and I was panting.

I remarked, "Regardless of how your hip is doing, your heart, lungs and feet sure seem in perfect marching order."

He growled, "Can't you keep up?"

"Barely!"

Suddenly, there was movement in the shrubbery and a rabbit appeared. It sprinted along the trail before it vanished back into the bushes. In a flash Rex started to chase the creature.

Sonderegger yelled, "Rex! *Fuss!*" and the dog stopped the chase immediately, turned around, and rushed back to the side of his master, as if the rabbit didn't exist.

I observed, "You have him well trained! Rex seems keenly obedient."

"What's the point in owning a dog if you can't control him? Mind you, Rex and I care for one another."

"I can see that!" And I asked, "How old is he?"

"Six," and he went on pensively, more to himself, it seemed, "and I plan to outlive him. Rex would be lost without me."

"I hope you do," I replied.

We got to a little stream and he slowed down a bit. I imagined that he used to lead his horses down to the creek to drink. The dog looked up at his owner.

The old man motioned with his head and said, "Sure, Rex. Go ahead."

The German shepherd ran into the stream and playfully jumped and splashed around in it. Then he ambled back toward us, shaking himself briskly.

My host said, "There's a log a little farther upstream where we can cross, or do you want to turn around and head home?"

I considered this, and then said, "I'd rather return. Erika might be looking for me."

He slowed his pace somewhat on our way back. I was not sure if he did so out of consideration for me or if he had tired a little himself. We treaded in agreeable silence for a while. I drank in the spectacular mountain scenery all around us and admired the view to the valley below.

Pointing to a mountaintop across the valley, I said, "If I'm not mistaken, that's the *Parsenn* over there?"

He replied, "Yes, that's the *Weissfluhjoch* and the *Parsenn* ski area."

"I wish I could be here in winter for skiing," I said dreamily.

"I know the feeling. In a couple of months I'll be longing for the first snowfall myself."

Surprised, I asked, "You still ski?"

"I sure do."

"What about your hip?"

"With the parabolic skis we use nowadays, one hardly has to move anymore. The shaped skis practically turn by themselves."

"Does your doctor agree with that logic?"

"I don't know. I didn't bother to consult him in the matter."

Then he questioned, "You still have a husband, I presume?"

"Yes, I have Peter."

"Did you leave him in America?"

"He's also in Switzerland. We separated for a week or so. Home base is in Zurich where my sister lives."

"I see. And what do you folks do when not traveling?"

"We both retired a while back."

"What? You're too young for a life of leisure. You're Erika's age."

"Actually, I'm a year older than her," I said, "but my husband and I are not idle. Peter writes books and I started a business."

"And what is that?"

"I named it R.A. Huber."

"Huber is your last name, so that doesn't tell me anything. Don't beat around the bush. What kind of business do you run?"

Reluctantly, I said, "I'm a private investigator."

He stopped in his tracks, looked me up and down, and then roared with laughter. I was not surprised at his reaction. I would have preferred to avoid the subject, but I knew he would not leave it alone, and that there was more to come.

Still amused, he said, "So you spy on unfaithful spouses and take pictures, et cetera?"

"No, I don't take on divorce cases."

"What kind of cases, then?"

"Having to do with crimes committed," I replied.

"Don't tell me you investigate murder!"

"Basically, that is mostly what I do."

He looked down at me disapprovingly, shaking his head.

"You think that is strictly a man's job, huh?"

"You've got that right!"

We did not speak for the next stretch, and the old man picked up speed again. I concentrated on keeping in step with him.

As we left the trail and the open field came into view, he nodded at his canine friend and said, "All right, Rex. Go for it!"

The dog took off like a bandit and soon came back with a stick in his fangs. Then they played the game of toss, fetch, and bring back to the master. I was content to just stand by and watch the activity. The perfect harmony between the man and his dog was heartwarming. I was wrong in thinking the conversation concerning my job was over and done with, however.

When we approached the mansion, he asked, "Where would you carry a gun?"

"Usually in my purse."

"Do you have it with you now?"

"I didn't bring my pistol to Europe. I'm on vacation."

"Good. You might hurt yourself with it!"

Then he looked at his watch and stated, "Perfect timing. I have a session with *Magic Fingers*."

Chapter 7

When Erika drove me back to the hotel in the early evening, she apologized, "So sorry I took so long with my work. I hope you weren't bored."

"Not at all. Your dad kept me entertained. His train room flabbergasted me! What a spectacular hobby he has created for himself there!"

"His trains are amazing, aren't they?"

"It must have taken him years to build the fantastic scene."

She nodded.

After a pause, she asked, "Did Papa behave himself?"

"Absolutely," I replied. "I enjoyed his company. We had some interesting conversations and even went for a walk."

"You mean a sprint!"

"Exactly! He appears to be in remarkably good shape."

"Oh he is. I'm sure he'll survive us all!"

I remarked, "At the moment he has a session with *Magic Fingers*. I assume that would be with the masseur?"

"No. That is what he calls Laura Thompson."

"And who is Laura Thompson?"

"You are going to laugh, but Papa is writing his memoirs."

"That doesn't surprise me. I can imagine he's led an interesting life, but what does this Laura Thompson have to do with it?"

"Papa hired her to take dictation, since he doesn't want to bother with the actual writing."

I said, "Oh, I see. This person is a ghostwriter."

"Not exactly," she replied.

"What is she, then?"

"She uses some kind of machine. It's hard to explain."

"Well, try! I have no idea what you're talking about."

"In your country, they have these reporters in a court of law, and - -"

"You mean from the press?"

"No, no, not from the newspapers. I mean the persons employed by the courts that take the procedures down. Help me out, Regula, what are these people called?"

"Oh! I get you now. You're talking about court reporters."

"Yes, that's it. Court reporters," she repeated.

"So this woman is a court reporter, and your dad hired her to record his memoirs on her steno-machine. Correct?"

"Precisely."

"Is Laura Thompson from the U.S.?"

"Oh, definitely. I don't think her profession exists here."

"And I'm sure your father dictates his memoirs in German. She must have an excellent command of the language."

"She does. Apart from a slight accent, she speaks it to perfection."

"Interesting. I hope I'll get to meet *Magic Fingers*."

Chapter 8

On the following day in the late afternoon, I sat on my room-terrace at Talblick and wrote postcards. I had purchased the cards in Aix-les-Bains, but never got around to addressing them. I wondered what my friends would think of the French postcards with Swiss stamps and postmarks.

My day had been interesting thus far. When I first arrived, Helga showed me to my room on the second floor. The large bedroom reflected natural lighting coming from the row of windows and glass door leading to the terrace. The blond pine furniture and the pure white comforter on the bed added to the sense of "fresh air" about the place. The adjacent bathroom looked new and luxurious.

As soon as I had unpacked, I went downstairs to explore the ground level of the mansion. I didn't get far, however. Walking along the hallway I spotted Rex sitting in front of a closed door. Another room off limits to the dog, I thought to myself.

At that moment the door was flung open and Otto Sonderegger, bare-topped, clad only in a towel around his waist, walked out. His torso seemed greasy or possibly sweaty.

I said, "Good morning, Mr. Sonderegger! I see you've had your massage."

"You're next!"

Behind the old man I perceived a big, muscular young man with blond hair and blue eyes.

My host introduced him as Hans Weber, and then stated, "Thanks to this fellow here my body is still functioning!" And he continued, "I was serious. Have a massage. You'll feel like new afterwards."

I shook my head and replied, "Not me. Thank you."

Winking, he said, "It's on the house. Just let Hans know when you're ready," and he passed by me. Rex got up and followed his master.

Left to myself, I reconsidered. Oh, why not? Every so often I suffered from lower back pain. A massage might not be such a bad idea. Besides, it would be a new experience for me. So minutes later, I found myself strolling back to the massage room.

Mr. Weber passed me in the hallway going in the opposite direction, his arms wound around a wad of dirty linens.

I asked, "Do you have time for me? I'm taking Mr. Sonderegger up on his offer."

"Uh-huh, wait in the massage room. Take everything off except your underpants."

What did I get myself into, I mused. This "Viking" of a man could crush me with two of his fingers!

The room was minuscule. Without the treadmill in one corner and the photo gallery on the walls, the place could easily have been mistaken for a patient room at a doctor's office. In the center stood an elongated piece of furniture similar to a physician's examining table. However, instead of the framed diplomas usually hanging in a doctor's examining room, these walls were adorned with black-and-white photos depicting past subjects and events at Talblick.

I undressed and sat down on the edge of the massage-table and was pleased to observe that the sheet draped over it looked fresh and clean. I found a towel hanging on a rack and wrapped it around my upper body. Then I gazed at the pictures. Many of them were of horses with or without riders. A few shots of tennis players holding trophies, presumably on the occasions of past tournaments held at Talbick, were displayed. There was a rather large picture of a dog chewing on a bone. Rex was not the object of this photo. It was a beautiful Alaskan husky.

I was just about to get up and have a closer look at the ski scenes on the far wall when the blond giant came back and said, "On your stomach, please."

As he started to rub lotion, - - or was it oil? - - on my back, I commented, "This is totally new for me. I've never had a massage before."

"Uh-huh."

"I don't know what to expect."

"Uh-huh."

While kneading my shoulders, he ordered, "You must relax your muscles."

Easy for him to say!

Then I asked, "How long have you been employed by Mr. Sonderegger?"

"Two years."

"Do you enjoy working for him?"

"Yes."

Then I inquired, "Do you make other house calls besides this one at Talblick?"

"No."

"So the other patients usually come to you for their massages?"

"Uh-huh."

"Where would that be?"

"Davos."

This was like pulling teeth! I could take a hint! Hans Weber was clearly not much of a conversationalist. In another moment I had lost all desire to talk as well. The young man so vigorously pounded and kneaded my back, all I managed to do was hold on to the sides of the table, close my eyes and pray for mercy.

At the end of the session I emerged from the massage room feeling like a truck had run over me.

Chapter 9

Strangely, by the time I had taken my second shower of the day washing the oil off my body, I felt relaxed and in a state of physical well-being. I had changed into shorts, a T-shirt and sneakers and planned a short jog. When I walked down the corridor once more, the door to one of the rooms stood open and I glanced inside. A young woman was working on a laptop computer. A steno-machine atop a tripod stood next to her chair. Aha, I deduced, this must be *Magic Fingers*.

I stood in the doorway and watched for a while. She was young, in her early twenties. Her brown hair was long and loosely tied into a ponytail at the nape. I saw her in profile; a strong forehead, straight nose, generously sized mouth and a gracefully long neck. She turned her face and as she looked up at me, I noticed that she was pretty.

"Can I help you?"

I introduced myself in English and added, "You must be Ms Thompson."

Her smile seemed sincere as she said, "Oh, of course, Mrs. Huber! Nice to meet you. My boss told me you were visiting. And please call me Laura."

I inquired, "You're a U.S. court reporter?"

"Sure am."

"From where?"

"Southern California."

"Me too!"

Excitedly she exclaimed, "Oh my gosh! Where do you live?"

"In Merida, a small town not too far from Pasadena. You've probably never heard of it."

"I've never been there, but it sounds familiar."

"How about you? Where is your home?"

"In Orange County on Balboa Island."

Enthused I said, "You live on Balboa! The small island is one of my favorite places. My husband and I usually park the car at the Newport Peninsula and then take the ferry across. We just love to stroll around amid the quaint, enchanting houses with cats sunning themselves in most front yards. I especially enjoy browsing and shopping in the boutique stores along Marine Avenue, as I always seem to be able to find chic outfits there. Some of the restaurants along the main drag offer excellent food. And of course, the magnificent view of Newport Bay along the front walk of the island is a treat in itself."

The young woman held up her hand and said, "Stop! You're making me homesick!"

"Sorry!" I said. "I just love that area."

Then I asked, "In which court were you employed?"

"Oh, I was a deposition reporter working for an agency. They sent me on jobs all over Orange County and beyond," she replied.

"I see. So Mr. Sonderegger hired you through your agency?"

"Actually, he found me by chance."

"Really?"

"It was last February. My aunt and uncle live in Davos, and they invited me for a ski vacation."

"Are your parents Swiss?" I asked.

"My mom is Swiss and my dad is American."

"Sorry for interrupting. Please go on."

"Anyhow, I was thrilled to be here and ski Davos. One evening my aunt and uncle gave a party. The guests were mostly older folks, and I wasn't interested in hanging around. So I excused myself and went to practice in the family room where there is a TV."

Puzzled, I said, "I don't understand. Practice what?"

"I always take my steno machine along on vacations and practice, so I don't lose speed."

"Interesting!"

She continued, "As I said, I went to the family room and tuned in to a talk show on TV. I wanted to see if I could take conversations down in German."

"Did it work out?"

"It was a struggle at first. They talked fast, but I got some of it." She went on, "One of the guests, Mr. Sonderegger, wandered into the room and apparently was fascinated with what I was doing. He made me explain the exact details of my work as a court reporter." She laughed as she recalled, "He even dictated a few sentences and then had me read them back to him."

"I can picture him insisting on that!"

"After that evening, I forgot all about him. Then, two days before I was scheduled to fly home he called and offered me a job to assist him with his memoirs. The suggestion came as a total surprise. I asked him for how long he would need me. He said as long as it'd take to write the memoirs. After thinking it over, I accepted his offer on a trial basis with the agreement that if there were problems, either one of us could cancel the deal after one month's time."

"Very wise of you. Obviously it seems to have worked out. You're still here!"

She nodded.

Motioning toward the tripod with the steno machine affixed, I said, "I would love to know the mechanics of it all, but I hate to impose on you any longer. I'm sure you're anxious to get back to work."

"Oh, I'm not busy at all today. I'm just editing and making corrections on what I took down yesterday. We had a short session, so I'm almost done. Give me five minutes and I'll be all yours." And she added, "Don't just stand in the doorway. Come on in and have a seat."

As she turned back to the computer, I made myself comfortable on an upholstered chair, the only one in the room aside from Laura's office chair. I presumed I had the "dictating" seat.

Five minutes later, true to her word, she said, "So what do you want to know?"

"How do you get the information from your steno machine to the laptop? Do you use a disk?"

"Yes. I need to use my German dictionary, obviously, when taking dictation from Mr. Sonderegger."

"I don't understand. How can you translate your machine strokes into German?"

"Let me show you," and while rummaging in a briefcase, she said, "I must admit that it took me several weeks to build up a dictionary by entering my keystrokes into the computer as German words."

She found an empty disk and inserted it into the side of her steno machine.

Then she said, "Okay, dictate something to me in German."

So I did. As her hands and fingers flew rapidly up and down, I realized that *Magic Fingers* was indeed an excellent name for her. Then she took the disk out of the machine and slid it into the laptop. After a few clickings and scrollings, the text I had dictated showed up on the computer screen.

"That simple!" I exclaimed.

Then I looked at the roll of paper that had come out of the steno machine while she had entered the info, and said, "So if what you're taking down goes directly onto the disk, what is the paper for?"

"That is just to read back at the spur of the moment. In court as well as during depositions, lawyers sometimes have you read testimony back to them before it is transcribed."

I looked at the tape of paper and asked, "You can read this? Looks like gibberish to me!"

"Steno is its own language. With the new technology we have now, the steno is automatically translated into English. However, in my case, I choose the German dictionary while I'm working here so that the strokes will translate correctly from Mr. Sonderegger's dictation."

"I think I understand now."

She went on, "The court reporter still has to edit the transcript, of course. Errors in strokes when taking the info down will prompt misspelling of words or even cause the strokes to be untranslatable." And she added, "The old manual steno machines were not computer compatible. One had to read from the paper and translate it into English and then type it manually into the computer in order to get a transcript."

I said, "I'm impressed with your skill. It must be difficult for you to take dictation in German since it's not your mother language."

"It can be challenging, but in a lot of ways it's easier than most jobs I was assigned to in the U.S."

"How come?"

"Well, Mr. Sonderegger dictates slowly. Sometimes he pauses for a long period of time to collect his thoughts. In the States, when I was taking down depositions the lawyers talked fast and on top of each other, especially when they got into arguments. They also were in a hurry to get the transcripts, so I was constantly under a lot of pressure."

"I bet that was stressful," I commented.

After a pause, I said, "Is Mr. Sonderegger easy to work for?"

"He's the *Dictator* and has to have everything exactly his way, but I like working for him. He pays me well and is generous in many other ways."

I liked her *Dictator* analogy. It occurred to me that Laura Thompson clearly was a witty young woman.

Then I asked, "Do you live at Talblick?"

"Well, when I first started on the job, my employer suggested that I do so, but I didn't take him up on it."

"For what reason?"

"Several, I guess. First of all, there is so much more for me to do in Davos. I'm young and I like to have some fun once in a while. I couldn't picture myself spending day and night with nothing but old people." She looked me in the eye, and said, "No offense, Mrs. Huber."

"None taken," I replied.

"I also enjoy living with my relatives. My aunt is a sweetheart, and we have a ball when my cousins come to visit. But I think the main reason is that I didn't want to become dependent on my boss."

"Good for you!"

Surveying the young woman, I remarked, "I can imagine your parents were upset when you stayed here instead of returning from your vacation."

"They didn't like it. But then, I'm an adult and can take care of myself," she said.

A thought came into my head, and I asked, "You *are* planning to go home? You're not thinking of staying in this country for good?"

"Oh, no. As soon as the memoirs are written, I'll go home."

"Any idea how long that will take?"

She grinned and said, "Your guess is as good as mine! We started last February and we're only on chapter 31. I'll be here for the next ski season and maybe even the one after that."

"Are they long chapters?" I inquired.

"Not particularly, but it's slow going. Mr. Sonderegger has me read back the manuscript every so often and makes a lot of changes and additions. Sometimes he has me delete an entire chapter and he starts all over."

"Are his memoirs about the hotel business or his private life?"

"Actually, both. I can tell he led an interesting life from what I've gathered so far." She chuckled, adding, "He was quite a womanizer in his time. I don't think he treated his first wife nicely, but then she was a hypochondriac and would have driven any man crazy."

She put a hand in front of her mouth, saying, "Gosh, that slipped out. I'm not supposed to talk about what's in the memoirs. Mr. Sonderegger doesn't want anyone to know about the contents until after they're published. I really don't know what came over me."

"I'll keep it a secret," I assured her. And I asked, "Does he always dictate in this room?"

"Most of the time, but if the mood so strikes him, we'll take the work elsewhere."

"For instance?"

"On a sunny day, he occasionally dictates out on the veranda or relaxing in the hammock, or even on his bedroom terrace."

"In other words, you're flexible."

"I can set up my tripod and steno machine anywhere and take down data, as long as I have a chair to sit on."

Then I inquired, "Do you work every day of the week?"

"It differs. Sometimes I do, and other times I hardly work all week long. My boss goes in spurts. When he's in the mood, he can dictate from morning till night, only taking time out to eat and go for a walk with Rex, for a few days in a row. Then again, it's not unusual for him to call me on a Sunday night with the news that I can have the entire week off. Other times he only dictates for an hour or so and then tells me I can go home after I'm done transcribing."

She snickered, "I'm done for today!"

"In that case you'd better get out of here, before your employer changes his mind," I said.

Chapter 10

I was ambling through the dining room and planned to exit onto the patio when I heard Erika's voice coming from the open kitchen door, "Is that you, Regula?"

I turned around and headed in her direction, saying, "Yep, it's me."

"Where are you going?"

"Jogging."

"Have some lunch first. I'll fix us omelets."

"Let me help."

"No, just sit down at the counter bar."

I grabbed a stool and then looked around. I was sitting at the huge counter aisle of an ultra modern, state-of-the-art kitchen. All the appliances were built-in: two ovens, a microwave and a rotisserie-grill against one wall and a dishwasher, stainless steel double-sink and refrigerator against another. The third was taken up with counter space. Cabinets were built over and below the long line of countertop. At the opposite side of the center aisle from where I was seated, a flat electric stovetop and another, smaller sink were built in. It was over this sink that Erika was standing, beating the omelet batter vigorously with a whip.

"Wow! What a kitchen!" I exclaimed.

"It's fairly new and plenty convenient. Helga loves it."

"Speaking of Helga," I remarked, "I'm amazed that she's still at Talblick."

"Yes, she has been loyal over the years."

"How old is she now?"

"She just turned seventy."

"I thought she was older than that. Not that she looks it, but after all, she was already here when we were kids."

Erika said, "I think she was very young when she started working for us, seventeen or eighteen, maybe."

"Over fifty years!" I marveled.

"You're right, she's been with us forever."

"Amazing that she lasted that long."

My friend chuckled. "What you meant to say is, it's amazing that she was able to tolerate Papa for that long!"

"I guess that occurred to me," I admitted.

"Just between you and me, I've always suspected that Helga is secretly in love with Papa."

"Ah, that might explain it. She never married?"

"Nope."

"By the way, where is she? I haven't seen her since she showed me to my room this morning."

"She went grocery shopping. We'll have some extra people for dinner tonight. The 'boys' are coming as per Papa's summons."

"I'm looking forward to seeing them."

The omelets were done and Erika poured us each a glass of iced tea.

After taking a couple of bites I commented, "Delicious! You've prepared them just right. I cook on gas burners at home, so I'd probably have scorched them on your electric stovetop."

"See! That's why I didn't want your help," she teased.

Then she said, "I hope you weren't too bored this morning, left alone. I have a deadline to meet and just needed to get some work done. I don't want to have to sit at the computer this weekend, since I'd like to take you to the village for the *Chilbi*."

"Please, Erika, you don't need to entertain me. Besides, I had an interesting morning."

"What did you do?"

"Well, I got my first massage, for one thing!"

"Did you like it?"

"When I left the massage room, I felt like every bone in my body had been dislocated, but a little later I felt relaxed. Now I'm energized and ready for some physical activity."

She said, "Hans Weber is clever with his hands."

"True, but he doesn't seem blessed with the gift of gab."

"You've noticed!"

"Honestly, is there anything in his vocabulary, besides 'uh-huh', 'yes', and 'no'?"

"Not much, I think."

I continued, "I also had a chat with Laura Thompson. She explained the entire fascinating process of court reporting to me. I was impressed with her. She seems mature for her age."

"I agree. She appears to know how to handle Papa. For his part, Papa seems to have taken an interest in her."

"She told me that she lives with relatives in Davos. Do they drop her off here? I'm sure she wouldn't take the train and walk up that steep hill on a regular basis."

"Funny you should ask. Early on, she used to ride up on a moped that she borrowed from her relations. Then one day she got caught in an unexpected storm. By the time she reached the house she was soaked to the bone. So Papa leased a car for her which she's been driving ever since."

"Generous of him," I commented.

When we had finished our lunch, I remarked, "I was going to jog, but I just had a better idea."

"What?"

"It seems a waste that your tennis court gets such little use. Let's play a couple of sets! What do you say?"

She raised her straight eyebrows and said, "You're joking?"

"I'm serious. I haven't played in years, but it'll be fun."

"I'm rusty myself."

"Come on, I'm sure you can find a couple of racquets and balls."

"Oh, that's not a problem, but - -"

"No 'buts' about it. Let's do it! See you on the court in half an hour."

I quickly got up, not giving her time for any protests, and walked out of the kitchen.

Chapter 11

When Erika joined me by the court, she was clad in white shorts, a white polo shirt and tennis shoes. She provided me with a racquet, opened a can of balls, and handed me two. Then she walked to the back of her court, and I headed to the rear of mine.

She hollered, "All right. Let's rally for a bit to warm up. Tell me when you're ready to start a game."

I made a thumbs-up sign.

My first attempts of keeping a rally going were pitiful. I had to force myself to swing slowly and keep arm and racquet straight. Wrist action and hacking at the ball with a sharp twist, like I was used to doing in racquetball, just would not do here. I was also having a hard time controlling the ball. Erika, on the other hand, seemed to return my sloppy shots effortlessly with well-placed groundstrokes. After rallying, we practiced our serves. At first mine went either into the net or ended up wide or long.

When I finally hit a couple of serves into the correct service box, she shouted, "Ready?"

I felt inadequate but knew that no amount of warming up would make a difference in the way I was going to play. So I nodded my head in assent.

As the game unfolded, it became even more obvious that my friend was the superior player. I noticed that she generally liked to play from the baseline. So I was able to score some points by hitting drop shots, which didn't give her enough time to run up to the net and get to the ball. By the time we were into our second set, I even managed to ace a couple of serves. We played two sets. Erika won 6-1 and 6-2.

As we walked away from the court, I uttered, "Rusty? Give me a break!"

She responded evasively, "I made some lucky shots."

"Luck had nothing to do with it."

She shrugged her shoulders.

I stood still, turned my face toward her and demanded, "Look me in the eye! What's going on?"

"I don't know what you mean."

"You've been playing tennis recently. I suspect you've done so on a regular basis. So what's the charade?"

She didn't answer and briskly walked ahead of me. I caught up with her, and as we got to the veranda, I said, "Please! Let's talk." Reluctantly, she dropped into a patio chair.

I sat down facing her and demanded, "Tell me what's going on!"

She looked in all directions. There was not a soul around except the two of us. Then she said, "All right. If you must know, I joined a tennis club in Davos at the beginning of the year. I wanted to do something just for me and away from Talblick."

"That's wonderful! But why the secrecy?"

"I don't want Papa to know."

After a pause, I said, "Is it that you don't want him to feel bad because he's not allowed to play anymore?"

"No, that's not the reason. I met someone at the club."

"So you met a man?"

"Yes."

"What's wrong with him?"

"Nothing's wrong with him. We're dating."

"I don't understand what going out with a man has to do with keeping your tennis playing a secret from your dad."

"Well," she said, "Papa knows some people at the club."

"So?"

"Normally folks avoid talking 'tennis' to him nowadays, but if he knew that I joined the club, he might bring the fact up himself when talking with the tennis cronies."

I shook my head and asked, "What exactly are you afraid of?"

"I'm not afraid of anything. I just don't want Papa to know I'm dating Claude."

"Do they know each other?"

"No, and I want to keep it that way."

I glanced at her pensively and then commented, "Erika, you are way past the age of needing your father's approval to date anyone. You are turning sixty next month, for heaven's sake!"

She snickered and said, "Thanks for remembering my birth date!"

"Don't evade the subject," I countered.

"Of course I don't need his approval. I just want to avoid any unpleasantness, that's all."

"Why should there be any unpleasantness, like you say?"

"Papa would certainly make fun of the relationship, and I don't want to expose Claude to any ridicule, nor myself, for that matter."

"Would there be anything to make fun of?" I inquired.

"Claude is a bit younger than me."

"How old is he?"

"Forty-five."

Then I asked, "Is the relationship serious?"

"Not yet," she answered, "but headed that way, I think."

We sat silently for a while, and then I said, "If your relationship with Claude progresses, you can't keep it a secret from your father."

"I'll cross that bridge when I get to it," she replied.

Chapter 12

I was still writing postcards when I heard the motor of a car and then observed a vehicle heading toward the old stables. My room was situated at the rear of the house and gave me a view in that direction. I got up and leaned on the terrace balustrade to get a better look. Soon a man and a woman with a teenage girl in tow emerged from the converted garage, each pulling a small suitcase on wheels. That must be Alex and his family, I deduced.

As they came closer and passed beneath my balcony, the woman waited for the girl to catch up, saying, "Lotti, stop pouting! Dad and I aren't thrilled to be here either, but we're trying to make the best of it. So you'd better do the same and stop complaining." The teen grumbled a reply, but by that time they had moved out of earshot.

I finally was down to my last card when another car was driving past the mansion toward the guest garage. This time a lone man exited the structure and walked to the house. At closer range he appeared to be in his early fifties, too old to be the son from Otto Sonderegger's second marriage. So this might be Norbert, I concluded.

It was getting a little chilly, and I checked my watch. A quarter till five already. I looked down at my shorts and T-shirt. Time to get cleaned up and ready for the evening, I decided, and went inside.

Chapter 13

I found Helga in the kitchen, chopping onions, and surveyed her for some time while she concentrated on her task. She had aged well, I thought. Her straight hair, now mostly gray, was cut in a short, flattering style. There were lines around the eyes and mouth area, and her chin was no longer firm, but she still had that competent look about her that I remembered from when she was young. She had gained a little weight around her middle, but she looked healthy and in shape. She wiped her hands on the apron and then looked up at me.

Noticing tears in her hazel eyes, I asked, "Are you all right?"

Perplexed, she replied, "Certainly!" Then she pointed at her eyes and explained, "Just the onions."

"Yes, of course. How stupid of me."

Then she commented, "You look lovely, Regula! That corn-blue suit you have on is becoming."

"Thank you! It's a slinky. One can throw these into a suitcase any which way, and they'll never wrinkle."

She scrutinized me some more and then said, "You've grown into an elegant woman." And chuckling she added, "A contrast to the tomboy you used to be!"

I asked, "What are you cooking?"

"Minced Veal a la Zurich."

"Can I help?"

"Nope, but come and sit at the counter and talk to me, if you have nothing better to do."

"I'd love to," I said, grabbing a stool.

She filled a big pot of water, threw in a handful of salt and placed it on the electric stovetop in the center aisle. I presumed she was going to boil the water for the noodles.

Then she wanted to know, "What have you been doing with yourself for the last forty years?"

I smiled and said, "I don't think you have time to listen to my biography! I'll try to tell you in a couple of sentences. You knew that I moved to the United States and then got married?"

She nodded.

"We have a daughter, as well as a son, and are blessed with three grandchildren. My husband, Peter, and I retired a while back. We both keep busy, though."

"With hobbies?" she asked.

"Of sorts. Peter took up writing and I started a second career. I'm in the sleuthing business."

"You're a private investigator?"

"Yes, I am."

She chuckled and said, "That sounds more like the Regula I remember! The chic woman somehow just isn't you."

"I like to combine the two." Then I stated, "Enough of me. Tell me about your life."

"It's the same as it always was," the housekeeper replied.

"I'm happy to still find you here, Helga. You haven't changed much!"

"The only difference is that I'm old," she said jokingly.

"You've spent your entire adult life at Talblick. I find that a big accomplishment."

"I've been here for fifty-two years, except for the few months I took care of my mother while she recovered from major surgery. During my absence the Sondereggers hired an Italian woman to take my place. With a twinkle in her eye she added, "I heard later that she was quite a looker but not much good in taking care of the household."

Then she said, "Overall, they were good years. I can't complain."

"I'm sure it wasn't always easy working for Mr. Sonderegger."

She grinned and said, "He can be difficult if he gets in one of his moods, but I've always been able to handle him."

She got the skillet ready for the veal, and I asked, "May I at least set the table?"

"I'll let you do that," she conceded. "Let me see, there will be" - - she counted on her fingers - - "Mr. Sonderegger, Erika, Alex, Mirella, Lotti, Norbert, and you: seven people."

"You don't eat with us?"

"Not when there are this many guests."

I made a few trips to and from the dining room, carrying plates, glasses, silverware and napkins. I was just about done setting the large table when Erika appeared at the door.

Surveying me doing my task, she said, "Thanks for helping, and while you're at it, add an extra place setting. Papa just told me that Fritz Moritz is staying for dinner."

"Will do. Who is Fritz Moritz?"

"Papa's friend. He's here a lot lately. He doesn't seem to know what to do with himself since his wife died," she replied.

Chapter 14

Alex Sonderegger, along with his wife and daughter, was the first to wander into the dining room. I would never have recognized him. We were both kids the last time we'd seen one another. The man who was approaching me now was in his late fifties. He was tall and broad. There was a slight resemblance between him and his father. They had the same gray eyes and a full head of hair. Alex's had now turned salt-and-pepper. But that was where the likeness ended. Whereas Otto Sonderegger gave the impression of being a commanding man with enormous willpower and aggression, his son appeared jovial and almost gentle, in spite of his big physique.

He said, "Regula! I wouldn't have known you if Erika hadn't told me you were visiting!"

"Nor would I have recognized you," I said as we embraced.

He introduced me to his wife, Mirella, and his daughter, Lotti. I judged Mirella to be in her forties. She had a slight accent and I presumed she was Italian. Her untamed dark, curly hair reached her shoulders, and her brown eyes sparkled with mischief. This woman was dynamite, I determined. Lotti had the same coloring, and I could picture her developing into a replica of her mother in a few years. At that moment, however, the teenager looked sulky and bored.

Erika and her younger brother appeared next. Norbert was fair with delicate features and blondish hair thinning at the crown, of medium height and thin.

He greeted his brother, sister-in-law and niece first. Then he walked over to me and formally said, "Welcome, Mrs. Huber!"

"What's this Mrs. Huber business? Don't be silly, Norbert. I'm the same Regula that gave you piggyback rides when you were three!"

He laughed and then gave me a hug, saying, "In that case, hi, Regula!"

We all sat down, and Alex announced, "I'm starving, I hope we don't have to wait for Papa much longer."

"He's in the train room with Mr. Moritz. They'll be here shortly," Erika put in.

Alex said, "He was playing with his trains when we first got here. Is he in there every day?"

"Pretty much," his sister answered. "He's working on a new project."

I heard approaching footsteps in the foyer and then Mr. Sonderegger's voice, "*Platz!*"

Obviously, Rex got the order to sit by the door. The two old gentlemen entered, and I was introduced to Fritz Moritz. I guessed that he was approximately the same age as our host, but not in as good shape. He walked carefully, supported by a cane. The small old man was impeccably dressed in a suit and tie, and though totally bald, he tried to make up for it by sporting a generous mustache.

He beamed at me and said, "Pleased to meet you!"

As soon as they were seated, Helga emerged from the adjacent kitchen and served salads followed by minced veal, noodles and green beans. The dinner conversation was pleasant enough at first, with Erika mostly providing the small talk.

Halfway through the meal, Mr. Sonderegger suddenly said, "You're probably all wondering why I asked you to come."

Alex, who was sitting next to me, murmured sarcastically, "No doubt to cheer us up!"

"What's that?" his dad bellowed.

"Never mind," replied Alex.

The old man continued, "I have an announcement to make, but since Karl isn't here yet, it'll have to wait until he joins us."

Norbert asked, "When will that be?"

"Tomorrow or Saturday."

"And after your announcement we can go home?"

The elder Sonderegger said sharply, "I told you all that I expect you to spend a few days at Talblick."

In a whiny voice Norbert replied, "I need to leave Monday or at the latest Tuesday. I have an auction to run in Basel."

His father said, "Stop your lamenting. You're just like your mother was, always whining!"

Irate, Norbert exclaimed, "How dare you talk about Mamma in that way? She was a saint! Outrageous, what she had to endure from you." And close to tears, he added, "You drove her into an early grave. She died of a broken heart!"

"Rubbish! We both know your mother died of pneumonia. Her heart, broken or not, had nothing to do with it."

After a short pause Mr. Sonderegger continued, "Why didn't you bring your partner?"

His son countered, "I will never have him come to this house again. You ridiculed him enough the last time."

The old man chuckled and said, "He was holding his own pretty well. As I recall, it was you who couldn't take the heat."

Norbert fell silent and his eyes started to get moist.

This seemed to enrage his father and he said, "If dear Mamma wouldn't have pampered you and brought you up as such a sissy, you might not have turned homosexual."

Alex put in, "Would you leave him alone, already?"

"Mind your own business. I'll deal with you later," the old man shot back.

There was an awkward silence, and then Lotti stated, "My teacher said that gay people are born that way. How they're brought up makes no difference."

The girl's grandpa raised his eyebrows at her and said, "Unbelievable what is taught in schools nowadays! I'd like to tell your teacher a thing or two. Why doesn't he stick to math, language, history and geography, rather than fill his students' heads with nonsense."

Mirella threw both arms up in the air and yelled, "*Basta, allora!*" meaning, "Enough already!" Then she continued in the Swiss-German dialect, "I will not have you criticize Lotti's teacher in front of her. You will apologize!"

Mr. Sonderegger, clearly enjoying himself, said, "Your Italian temper is evident, my dear Mirella. If I were a few years younger, I'd be aroused by it!"

She glared at him, and if looks could kill, the old man would have dropped dead instantly. Alex clenched his fists until the knuckles turned white.

I felt uncomfortable sitting in on the family quarrels. However, I was curious to see each person's reaction. It would have been too obvious to look Alex straight in the face since he sat right next to me, but I noticed he slowly started to unclench his fists. Mirella was still fuming, judging from the dangerous sparks in her eyes. Lotti had gone back to looking bored. Norbert stared into his plate. As I glanced toward Erika, we made eye contact and her gaze was full of apologies. Mr. Moritz was busily devouring his food, not looking up at anyone. The only person in the group totally at ease seemed to be Mr. Sonderegger, seated at the head of the table. As our eyes met, he had the gall to wink at me!

Then he raised his wine glass with exaggerated Italian mannerism, proclaiming, *"Saluti tutti!"* in other words, "Cheers to all!"

The remainder of the meal passed without further incident. Alex, the banker, discussed current interest rates and such. Erika talked about the carnival coming to the village, and Norbert elaborated on the apparently exquisite antiques being auctioned off in Basel the following week. Mr. Moritz challenged his friend to a game of chess after dinner.

The meringue-glacé Helga offered for dessert looked tempting, but I declined. I complimented her on the excellent dinner and then excused myself from the table.

Chapter 15

I was sitting on a patio chair looking up at the bright stars. What a glorious, clear summer night near the mountains! Then I beheld the valley below with the clusters of lights reflected from Dörfli and, farther down, the vast sea of brilliance spotlighting the entire area of Davos. Knowing I would be out here after dinner, I had previously set my tiny silver travel-ashtray with cigarettes and lighter on the veranda table.

Moments later, Erika stepped out and said, "Oh, here you are. What on earth are you doing sitting in the dark?" as she switched on the outdoor lights.

"Just enjoying the splendid evening," I replied.

She glanced at the table and said, "You're well equipped! You could've stayed for coffee and dessert. We have ashtrays in the house, you know."

"I wouldn't do that. I don't think there are any smokers in your family."

She sat down next to me and replied, "Karl smokes. You'll have a partner in crime, once he gets here."

"Touché!"

Then she said, "I'm sorry about the dinner episode. Typically, like always at family gatherings, Papa amused himself by mocking everyone."

"Why are they coming, then, if it seems such an ordeal?"

"One does not say 'no' to a summons from Papa."

"Why not?"

She gave me a look and said, "What do you think?"

"Are they that worried he might disinherit them?"

"Naturally."

I asked, "Would your dad really do that?"

"Probably not," she replied, "but you never know with Papa." And she continued, "Some years ago when he went through one of his fits, he threatened to divide his fortune equally between Helga and me and leave nothing to the boys."

"I see. So his snide remarks are primarily directed at your brothers and stepbrother?"

"Mostly, but he can have his fun with me too. He'll attack anyone when so inclined."

We sat in silence for some time. Then she remarked, "You're going to laugh at me, but I believe that Papa is at his worst behavior during a full moon."

I glanced at the sky and stated, "It's almost full now."

She grinned and said, "In that case the worst is yet to come!"

Then I asked, "Did he really treat your mom as badly as Norbert seems to imply?"

"He didn't treat her nicely, but then she asked for it, I think."

"Really?"

Erika gave me another of her looks and then inquired, "How well do you remember Mamma?"

"Not well, but I do recall that she was a fair beauty in a rather delicate way."

"Exactly!"

"What do you mean by that?"

She said, "Mamma played on being 'delicate.' Any little task was too much for her. Don't get me wrong, for I loved her dearly, and she was a good mom. She had a lot of patience, especially with Norbert. She seemed to bring out the worst in Papa, however."

"Because they were so different?"

She nodded, "You know how Papa loves to play sports and welcomes any challenging task. Mamma was just the opposite. She was totally disinterested in sports activities and shied away from anything daring."

I asked, "Norbert seemed to have admired her a great deal?"

"He worshiped her! I suspect she took him into her confidence in the last two years of her life, which was a mistake."

"I don't think I understand," I said.

"One should never take a child into one's confidence, especially not a sensitive boy like Norbert was."

"I get that part."

My friend explained, "As things got worse between my parents, Mamma became sort of a recluse. She also shed a lot of tears, which of course infuriated Papa. He hates any kind of weakness. So she used Norbert for a shoulder to cry on."

"I see." And I asked, "How old was Norbert when she died?"

"Thirteen."

"Poor boy, her passing must have hit him hard."

She nodded.

"Must not have been easy for you and Alex, either. He was sixteen and you were nineteen at the time."

She nodded again.

Then I asked, "When did your father marry his second wife?"

"A couple of years later," she replied.

"I was already in the States and consequently never met her. What was she like?"

Erika smiled and shared, "She was a lot of fun. We were the same age and got along great."

"You and your stepmother are the same age?"

"Yes, we were twenty-one when Papa married her."

"Did the boys also accept her that well?"

"Alex did, but Norbert never appeared to accept her at all."

I remarked, "You didn't live at Talblick much longer after your dad remarried. If I remember correctly, your own wedding was soon afterward."

"That's right, I married about a year later, but I came to visit a lot after my Stefan was born. Our two babies were almost the same age."

"I've lost you, Erika. What two babies?"

"Karl and Stefan were born one month apart."

"I know that your dad has a son named Karl out of his second marriage, but I didn't realize he had been the same age as Stefan." And I added, "According to your father, Karl is expected soon, so I'll get to meet him. What is he like, by the way?"

"Charming, but absolutely up to no good!"

Then I said, "You've lived with your dad for the past fourteen years, you must be getting along fairly well or you wouldn't stay."

She considered and replied, "I've never thought about it, but yes, overall we get along." She paused and then continued, "He was good to me after I lost Robert and Stefan. I was in shock for a long time and barely functioned for the first year. Papa practically forced me to take classes and become a programmer. As it turned out, that was the best thing for me, almost therapeutic."

"A good choice. Fourteen years ago computer programmers were in demand and you were young enough to easily absorb new concepts."

I glanced at her and said, "I'm sorry. I've brought disturbing memories back for you."

"I don't mind. I've been fine for years now."

We didn't speak for some time, each left to our own train of thoughts.

I finally asked, "Do you know what announcement your father was talking about?"

"I haven't the slightest idea, but I'm sure it will be dramatic," she answered.

Chapter 16

Before leaving Zurich I had borrowed my sister's cell phone so Peter and I could stay in contact. He called me on that Thursday evening, and I was pleased to hear the familiar voice say, "Hi! Where are you?"

"Hello, Peter! I'm at Erika's. And where are you calling from?"

"Neuchâtel, staying with Jean-Pierre and Annette."

"Are you enjoying yourself?"

"I'm having a ball!" And he went on, "We just finished dinner and plan to go out on the town later."

I glanced at my watch and remarked, "It's already 9:30, you party animals!"

He chuckled and said, "Jean-Pierre doesn't fully come to life until about midnight or so."

Then he asked, "Are you having a good visit with Erika?"

"Definitely. She is the same old sweetheart. At the moment she's preoccupied with her job, but she'll make time for me on the weekend. Until then, I have plenty of ways to amuse myself here."

"How?"

"I've had two interesting days," and I gave him a short version of my experiences at Talblick, ending with the dinner conversations of that evening.

He listened to my narrative and then said, "Sounds like the old man is still pulling all the strings, huh?"

"Absolutely."

"Was he mean to you when you walked with him and his dog?"

"Not at all. He's an autocrat, of course, but I enjoyed his company."

"So he mainly has a gripe with his sons?"

"Or anyone that crosses him, I would assume."

"Do you know what the sons have done to cause his hostility?"

I explained, "None of them wanted to get into the hotel business and eventually take over the Sonderegger dynasty."

Peter cackled, "Dynasty? Come now! Owning a hotel in Davos can hardly qualify a person as the ruler of a dynasty."

"He didn't only own the one in Davos. He had accumulated a bunch of hotels in other resort areas and major cities all over Switzerland."

"I see." And he asked, "I guess he is retired now and hired himself some top notch people to run the business?"

"No, he sold all the hotels."

"The old boy must be filthy rich, then."

"Otto Sonderegger is enormously wealthy."

"I can understand that the guy is disappointed that his business is no longer in family hands, but he seems to carry an exaggerated grudge. I mean, from what you told me, the way he taunted his gay son at dinner seems excessive."

"True." And I added, "I feel sorry for the man."

"You're talking about the son, right?"

"I didn't mean Norbert."

Peter sounded incredulous as he asked, "You feel sorry for Otto?"

"Yes, I do."

"Explain that one to me!"

"Well, I think it's rather sad that the old gentleman's only way of keeping his family around is by their fear of being disinherited if they don't abide by his wishes."

"I wouldn't have looked at it that way, but maybe you're right." And he added, "I believe you actually like your autocrat!"

"I admire him for what he accomplished and for the quality of life he still manages to enjoy. After all, he built up his hotel empire by hard work and a good business sense. And now that he no longer can participate in his favorite sport activities, instead of feeling sorry for himself, he got his hip functioning again by sheer willpower and physical therapy. By the way, the "Train-Disneyland" he created for himself borders on genius! On top of that, he is writing - - or, rather, dictating - - his memoirs."

After a pause Peter asked, "How long are you planning on staying there?"

"Until Sunday or Monday. They're having the carnival in the village this weekend."

"You mean *Chilbi*?"

"Of course."

"I haven't been to one since I was a child."

"Neither have I."

Then he asked, "Where are you going next?"

"Probably Bad Ragaz," I replied. "How about you? Are you driving to Geneva tomorrow?"

"Yes, I'll have a leisurely drive over in the afternoon. The convention doesn't start until evening. I'll call you as soon as I have a hotel telephone number."

I heard some background noise as Peter said, "We'd better hang up, they're waiting for me. Good-night, Hon!"

"Good-night. Love you!"

Just before cutting the connection, I said, "And Peter, you guys behave yourselves!"

Chapter 17

I slept soundly in my comfortable feather bed that first night at Talblick and dreamt of mountains, trains, waterfalls, and the giant, grinning face of Otto Sonderegger looming above it all. Waking up, I took some time to realize that the sound I heard was not from a train rushing by, nor the steady flow of a waterfall, but was coming from a vacuum cleaner in some room nearby.

I opened my eyes and squinted at the digital clock on the nightstand. Heavens! It was almost 9:00 a.m.! I stepped out onto the terrace. The promise of another fine day was in the air. At home in Southern California, I was used to taking fair weather for granted, but in Europe sunshine was a gift.

Three quarters of an hour later, showered and groomed, I heard a knock at my door.

"Yes?"

A woman with a scarf pulled over her head looked in, saying, "Oh, sorry! I'll come back later."

Surprised, I asked, "Do you need something from this room?"

"Oh, no," she answered, "I just wanted to vacuum and dust. I'm Rita Schmied, the cleaning woman."

"I'm R.A. Huber. Come on in."

"I don't want to bother you. I'll come back later."

"You're not bothering me, but I don't think the room needs cleaning; I've only spent one night."

She entered and looked around. Her eyes swept the room and remained fixed on the bed for a split second longer. She obviously checked if I had made up the bedding correctly.

Then she suggested, "Maybe just a little dusting."

I made a gesture encircling the room and said, "Go ahead."

I surveyed her while she attacked the place with her feather duster. She appeared to be in her fifties. Her face was round and the frizzy hair escaping from the scarf was brownish, mixed with gray. Although a chubby little woman, her movements were swift and agile.

Tucking a lock from her forehead back under the scarf, she self-consciously remarked, "I just got a perm and the curls turned out too tight."

"Give it a few days, and the waves will relax."

She rested the duster on her hip and, giving me a scrutinizing look, stated, "I heard about you. You're Mrs. Graff's friend, and you live in America."

"You heard correctly."

By this time she seemed finished with the dusting. She walked over to the bathroom door, opened it and looked around the place, closed the door again, and then turned to me, commenting, "You're neat. I can't see a thing that needs doing in there. Do you want fresh towels?"

"No thanks, they're perfectly fine to use again."

She lingered on, and just to make conversation, I asked, "Have you worked here long?"

"Six years already."

"You're not a live-in, I take it?"

"No, I live in Dörfli with my husband. I only come to clean twice a week. On Mondays I do the downstairs and on Fridays the upstairs."

"It's a big house. I can understand that it takes a full day to clean just one level."

"That's right."

She still made no attempt to leave, and I realized the woman clearly enjoyed a break from her work.

She remarked, "When I was young, I worked for the Sondereggers as a live-in maid. My parents weren't too happy about it, though. They'd have preferred I'd made an apprenticeship and learned a trade, but I wanted to earn money straight after I'd completed the mandatory schooling. So I worked here as a maid until I got married. Now that all my kids have left the nest, I took this cleaning post to make some extra money."

"So you like working for Mr. Sonderegger?" I asked.

"Sure, I'm used to him. I mostly take orders from Helga Hodler, the housekeeper, though. The work isn't hard nowadays with only Mr. Sonderegger, Mrs. Graff and Miss Hodler around. Once in a while there are guests, but that's nothing compared to the parties and the amount of people that were entertained here in the old days."

I said, "I can imagine life was pretty busy at Talblick in your live-in days?"

"You can say that again! There were the boys to clean up after, especially Karl, the youngest. He left a mess behind wherever he wandered. He was a holy terror too! Mr. and Mrs. Sonderegger gave lavish parties, so there were always people coming and going in those days."

I interrupted her flow and asked, "You are talking about the second Mrs. Sonderegger, correct?"

"Of course. I never knew the first one. She was before my time."

"The second lady of the house was after mine."

She remarked, "A good-looking woman and temperamental. Mr. Sonderegger sure knew how to pick them." Clearly enjoying herself, she took a step closer to me and continued with her gossip, "He had an eye out for the ladies. He was a handsome devil then. I was attracted to him myself, but I knew my place," she stated, full of virtue.

Then she said, "I'd better get back to work. You're sure you don't want me to vacuum?"

"Positive," I assured her.

"Well, have a nice stay, Mrs. Huber." That said, she walked out the door.

Chapter 18

Before I went downstairs for breakfast, I looked in on Erika. Her bedroom was also located on the second floor. When I knocked on her door and got no answer, I tried the office adjacent to her room and saw that she was busily typing on her computer.

Looking up, she said, "Regula! Did you sleep well?"

"Like a baby! I see you're already hard at work."

"Not really. I was checking if there were any decent seats left for the concert. Would you like to hear a Bach and Mozart concert tonight?"

"I'd love to!"

"Good! Let me quickly reserve the tickets," she said, and her fingers ran over the keyboard once more. At the end of the transaction she remarked, "I was also going to take you out to dinner in Davos before the concert, but Papa informed me that Karl is expected to arrive at any moment. So he wants us all here for the meal tonight."

"Oh, yes. To make his mysterious announcement."

Then she said, "I'm sorry, but I have to work some more today. I'll be all yours by this evening and on the weekend, though."

"Don't worry about me. I can entertain myself," I stated, and left her to get on with her job.

Chapter 19

Downstairs, as I walked along the hall, I heard Mr. Sonderegger's strong voice coming from what I called the "dictating room." The door stood open and when I passed by, I got a glimpse of *Magic Fingers* busily stroking her machine while the boss was seated in the upholstered chair across from her. Rex lay happily sprawled out at his master's feet. Apparently, this was a room the canine was allowed to be in, I observed. It also occurred to me that if Mr. Sonderegger was so keen on keeping his memoirs a secret until after publication, dictating them in his loud voice with the door open was defeating his purpose!

Twenty minutes later, fortified with a typical Swiss breakfast of bread, butter, preserves and cheese, I opted to go for a stroll. Having consumed a late breakfast, I planned to skip lunch. I had passed the patio and came upon Lotti relaxing in the hammock. She had a laptop propped up on her knees, and getting closer, I noticed she was playing a computer game.

"Hi! Are you winning?"

"Trying to," she answered, without looking up.

I surveyed the screen while she hacked at the keyboard. The game involved some sort of karate fighting figures of both sexes jumping into action. It looked totally confusing to me.

I commented, "This game is a far cry from Pac-Man, Mappy or Dig Dug!"

She rolled her eyes but never averted them from the screen and kept playing. When the game was over she checked her e-mail inbox, then exited out of the Internet and shut down the laptop.

She said, "Nobody sends me any messages. My friends are all away on vacation."

"Which is normal in August, I would think."

"Yeah, I wish I was somewhere on a trip too."

"You're on vacation right here at Talblick."

"Whoopee!" she blurted out sarcastically.

"Look at the bright side. No school and no homework! Besides, I think it's a lovely spot to be at."

"Yeah, but there's nothing to do." And she continued, "When Opa kept horses, I could at least ride. Now there isn't even that."

"Don't you like his train room?"

"Sure, it's cool, but Opa has to be at the controls himself. He doesn't let me handle them anymore since last year."

"What happened?"

She admitted, "I purposely crashed two trains into each other so that they derailed. He was furious and won't let me touch the controls ever again."

"You can't really blame him."

She shrugged. "I guess not."

Then I said, "I'm sure your family is taking other vacations, besides coming here."

"Of course, but every summer Opa wants us to come for at least a week, sometimes longer. The winter-sport stay in February is actually fun. I love snowboarding." She went on, "He makes us come for weekends at other times too. I especially hate his boring tennis tournaments in the spring."

"You don't play tennis?"

"I hate tennis. My hand-eye coordination is off. I'm lousy at tennis."

I thought there was nothing wrong with her hand-eye coordination when it came to computer games, but I refrained from commenting.

After a pause, she shared, "My brother is lucky this time. He has the perfect excuse for staying away. He's in the *Rekrutenschule.*"

"Oh, that's right, you have an older brother. He must be twenty if he's in military training."

She nodded.

"I don't remember, for how long is the *Rekruten-schule?*"

"21 weeks, and he just started," she replied.

"What profession has he decided on?"

"Engineering. He's not finished with his education yet."

"So he didn't want to go into the hotel business?"

"No way! He had a big fight with Opa about it. Opa wanted him in the business badly."

After a pause, I asked, "How old are you, Lotti?"

"Fifteen."

"Did your grandpa ever approach you about eventually taking over his hotel business?"

"Of course not. He's a male chauvinist. He would've never wanted a woman to run his business."

"I see."

With a touch of humor she said, "I'm glad he didn't. This way I wasn't forced to say 'no' to him!"

She seemed lost in thought for a while, and then said, "I wonder who's adopted? Do you know?"

"What are you talking about?"

"When I came down the hallway earlier, I heard Opa dictate. He said something about an adoption agency. So I'm curious as to who was adopted. Maybe it's Aunt Erika or Uncle Norbert. I don't think it's Dad, since he looks like Opa." Then she giggled and said, "Wouldn't it be funny if it turned out to be me!"

I said, "I wouldn't speculate if I were you. The mention of an adoption agency might have nothing to do with your family."

She shrugged and said, "I stopped at the open door and was going to ask him, but he didn't give me a chance. He frowned and criticized the way I dress. So I got mad and walked away."

I looked at her outfit. The low-rider jeans reached barely below her hipbones, and with her spaghetti-strap top ending a couple of inches beneath her chest, there was plenty of skin showing above and below her navel. Not my idea of chic elegance, but with her lean, young body, she could carry it off.

I pointed at her outfit and stated, "Some teenagers and young women I've seen dressed in this fashion would be better off covering up their bellies, but you, my dear, have the perfect figure for it."

Clearly pleased, she said, "Well, thank you!"

Then she sighed and remarked, "The worst thing about being here is that I can't talk to my friends. I've tried to reach some on my cell phone, but they must've shut theirs off while away on trips." And she added regretfully, "There aren't any boys either."

"Maybe you'll meet boys your age at the *Chilbi* tomorrow."

She grimaced and countered, "Yeah, probably all hicks."

Amused, I observed, "And that won't do for a city girl like you, huh?"

Then I said, "I'm going for a walk. Care to join me?"

She looked at me as if I'd lost all my marbles to suggest something that boring. However, she answered politely, "I'm waiting for my parents. We're going to Davos to do some shopping."

"Sounds like fun!"

"I don't know what's taking them so long. Either Dad's checking the stock market, or Mom is taking forever to put on her makeup."

"Well, have a great time shopping. See you at dinner," I said, and took off in the direction of the former stables.

Chapter 20

The idea that there were no more horses at the Talblick paddocks was still hard for me to fathom. As I strolled abreast of the structure, my curiosity got the best of me and I took a peek inside. No expense had been spared to convert the stables into a well-designed guest-parking garage. It was constructed similarly to public parking structures, with a passageway leading to a row of eight marked spaces providing for parking cars side by side. This way, no parked vehicle could be blocking any of the others. At that time, four cars were parked. I examined them and amused myself with a guessing game of matching the wheels to the owners. I assumed that Otto Sonderegger, Erika, and Helga used the mansion's attached garage. So I allotted the big blue SUV to Alex's family, the silver BMW to Norbert, the little white Toyota to the court reporter, and the old Fiat to the cleaning lady or possibly the masseur.

I chose to take a different trail from the one Sonderegger had taken me the other day. This path went along the edge of the plateau and allowed for yet another magnificent view of the valley. I must have hiked for about a quarter mile when the trail curved and led away from the edge. As the terrain was getting more and more rugged, I felt glad I was wearing tennis shoes. When I approached the little stream, I realized that I had been circling the entire Talblick estate. In order to get to the mansion without turning around, I had to cross the creek, so I found a spot where the stream narrowed and jumped. I had misjudged the distance, or possibly my jumping ability was not what it used to be. Whatever the reason, I landed short of the bank and got a shoe full of muddy water.

For the remainder of the hike I was aware of my soggy sock and shoe with every step I took, and by the time the mansion came into view, I was practically limping. From a distance I could tell that someone else had taken Lotti's place in the hammock. As I approached, I observed a young man lounging in it.

He asked, "Are you lost?" And surveying me more attentively, he added, "Looks like you fell into the creek!"

"Sure did," I admitted.

Then he stated, "This is private property," and with a most engaging grin he continued, "You look pretty harmless, so I might let you pass through!"

His pretense of being the owner of the estate amused me. I was looking at a handsome man in his thirties, with dark curly hair, brown, humorous eyes and the most appealing smile. His tremendous charm was not lost on me, but by the same token I had the feeling that I could not trust him an inch.

I said, "I'm R.A. Huber. I'm on the premises at Otto Sonderegger's invitation."

"Oh, sorry." And chuckling he continued, "Amazing how he still has an appetite for the ladies, at his age!" Then looking me up and down, he commented, "Not a bad choice!"

I decided this had gone far enough and felt compelled to set him straight.

So I said, "You must be Karl Sonderegger, and you're jumping to the wrong conclusion. I am not your father's lover. I'm Erika's friend."

He glanced at me meekly and said, "So sorry! I do apologize." And eyeing my wedding ring, he said, "Please forgive me, Mrs. Huber."

"You're forgiven," I uttered generously.

After a pause I pointed at his bag, tossed carelessly beneath the hammock, saying, "You must have just arrived?"

"Yeah, I parked the car, and this is as far as I got. I haven't been inside to greet Papa nor anyone else yet. The hammock looked too inviting! Once I enter the house, the arguing might start."

"In that case, enjoy the peace and quiet. As for me, I'd better change into dry footwear," I remarked while passing by him.

Chapter 21

As an afterthought, I had thrown my prepared-for-anything simple little black dress into my small suitcase when I repacked in Zurich. Now it came in handy. I wore it to dinner that Friday evening, since Erika and I were to take off for the concert afterwards.

As expected, the entire family was present, with me being the only outsider. A pleasant aroma escaped through the adjacent kitchen door when Helga carried the steaming food to us.

Norbert exclaimed, "Helga! You cooked my favorite: meatloaf, red cabbage, mashed potatoes and gravy!"

The housekeeper smiled at him and said, "I sort of had you in mind when I decided on the menu."

Erika started to introduce me to Karl, but he quickly said, "Mrs. Huber and I have already met. We had a most pleasant chat." And he grinned at me mischievously.

Then no one spoke. We kept busy concentrating on the tasty food. Mr. Sonderegger, seated at his usual place at the head of the table, seemed in an agreeable mood and surveyed his family with benevolence, it appeared.

Toward the end of the meal he addressed his youngest son, "It's about time you showed up."

"I came as soon as I could get away," Karl retorted.

"Get away from what? Do you have a paying job, then?"

"I started a business, but it didn't work out. I soon had to give it up."

His father said, "Another one of your shady deals, I presume."

"It was perfectly legit. I just wasn't successful, that's all," his son shot back.

"Easier to live off women, isn't it?" Not getting a reply, Mr. Sonderegger continued, "Are you still staying with that woman in Zurich?"

"No, Papa. I moved on."

"In other words, you got thrown out. Sooner or later the women get wise to you." Then he said, "Speaking of women, how is your mother doing?"

"Wonderfully. She's on an Alaskan cruise as we speak," Karl replied.

"Dear Esmeralda never liked to stay in one place for too long. I still miss her, you know!"

His son shot him a look and said, "Why do you persist in calling her Esmeralda? Her name is Maria, so call her by her name!"

Chuckling the old man said, "Esmeralda suits her so much better, don't you think? After all, she's got Gypsy blood in her!"

Apparently, Karl decided to humor him as he answered, "That must be where I get my wanderlust from."

Mr. Sonderegger's expression turned serious as he continued, "Well, we've all been waiting for you. Now that you're here, I can make my announcement." He paused dramatically and then stated, "I am making a new will, and - -"

I stood up and said, "This is obviously a family matter. Please excuse me."

Before I got halfway to the door, he stopped me, commanding, "Get back here and sit down. I have nothing to hide from you, Regula."

Reluctantly, I took my seat again as he went on, "Like I said, there is a new will. Since my sons took no part in helping build up the hotel business - - and it goes without saying that my entire fortune is a product of that business - - I see no reason why they should benefit from it after my death."

Alex was clenching his fists again as the old man elaborated, "I have made provisions of a certain sum for Erika, and a lesser amount for Helga. There is also a legacy for my friend Fritz. If I feel so inclined, I might change my mind and make provisions for any or all of you men at a later time. As it stands, the bulk of my estate goes to Laura Thompson."

The bombshell was out! There was total silence in the room. Everyone seemed in shock. Alex, seated next to me, slowly unclenched his fists. Mirella's eyes gleamed dangerously. Lotti was carefully chewing her food, the only person in the room still able to eat. Norbert had turned white as snow and looked like he might get sick. As I glanced at Erika, I noticed compassion and sadness showing in the gray eyes beneath the straight brows as she looked at her brothers. Surprisingly, a faint smile appeared on Karl's lips. I wondered what he could be thinking of. My attention finally turned back to our host. He was staring at his sons, one by one, keenly noting their respective reactions.

Lotti was the first to speak. She turned to Alex and said, "We really don't need the money, do we, Daddy?"

Alex answered her, "You're missing the point. This is a blatant insult to our family."

Norbert, having regained some color in his face, said, "Exactly. We are his flesh and blood, and he leaves his money to a stranger."

Mirella fixed her eyes accusingly on Karl and asked, "What are you grinning about?"

He replied, "I'm planning my own strategy."

"Such as?"

"It occurred to me that I could get on the good side of the lovely Miss Thompson. I met the woman this afternoon, and the prospect of wooing her is a pleasant thought."

Norbert interjected, "You are disgusting!"

I glanced at Otto Sonderegger and perceived that he seemed to enjoy the show.

At that precise moment, the door abruptly was flung open and Mr. Moritz, clearly in a state of agitation, advanced toward the head of the table.

He came to a halt in front of his pal, and, pointing his metal cane at him in a menacing manner, shouted, "You bastard! I thought we were friends! You dirty - -"

Mr. Sonderegger interrupted, "Calm down, Fritz. You know that getting this upset will raise your blood pressure sky high."

"The hell with my blood pressure. You lousy piece of shit! Seducing my Anna while I looked up to you and considered you my best friend. You will pay for this, I swear!"

The little old man was totally beside himself. His face was bright red and I was afraid that, indeed, the man's blood pressure must have been at a dangerously high level.

Perplexed, his friend said, "But, Fritz, that was thirty years ago!"

"That doesn't make it hurt any less."

"Do you mean you just found out?"

The little man nodded.

"How?"

Mr. Moritz struggled to gain control and then said, "Now, two months after Anna's death, I finally got up the courage to sort through some of her things. I came across her diary, and - -"

At this point he broke off, overwhelmed by emotion.

Otto Sonderegger said, "Leave it to a woman to keep a diary and confess her sins in it!"

This remark was obviously the last straw for Mr. Moritz. He first raised the cane at his friend again, and then thought better of it, turned around, and heading for the door, shouted, "I never want to see you again!" When he passed by us, he seemed to notice for the first time that other people were present.

Clearly embarrassed, he murmured, "Sorry for the intrusion."

Mr. Sonderegger appeared stunned for a moment, and then he got up and chased after his friend. When he was in the hallway we could hear him yell, "Fritz, wait! Be reasonable. I'm sorry you found out this way."

Chapter 22

While waiting for Erika to change, I went to my room to refresh my makeup. I was applying a final touch of lipstick when Peter called.

He gave me his Geneva number and then said, "I can't talk for long since I have to be at a meeting soon."

"Neither can I. Erika is taking me to a concert shortly." And I briefly informed him of our dinner drama.

He said, "I bet it was awkward for you to sit through the new will announcement."

"It was extremely uncomfortable."

"The scene with the old man's friend must have been embarrassing too."

"Sure was!"

"You're not going to stay there much longer, are you?"

I replied, "I want to experience the carnival tomorrow, but I think on Sunday I'll head for Bad Ragaz. By Monday or Tuesday I'll be ready to travel back to Zurich."

"Oh, I hadn't planned to get to Zurich before Wednesday or possibly Thursday," he said.

"Take your time, Peter," I assured him. "After all, I grew up in Zurich. There's plenty for me to do until you join me."

At that moment Erika stuck her head in, saying, "Ready?"

I quickly spoke into the phone, "Got to run! Good luck with the convention. I hope you'll get lots of networking in! Love you!" And we hung up.

Chapter 23

I stood outside the mansion and looked up at the sky. In another night or two there would be a full moon, I observed. Erika pulled the car out of the garage, and I got in. She concentrated on driving as we wound down the curvy road, lit only by our headlights.

When we were entering the main road of Dörfli, she said, "Look, they're setting up for the carnival. It will be slow going for a mile or so, but don't worry. We'll make it on time."

Soon we were stuck in a caravan of trucks, vans and what looked like circus wagons. Traffic was moving at a snail's pace. Neither one of us felt like talking, it seemed.

Erika finally broke the silence and said, "You must think we are a totally dysfunctional family." And she continued, "We're not always this bad, you know."

"Of course not. My visit coincided with a particularly trying time for you folks," I replied.

"I'm sorry you had to be a witness to it all. I wish Papa would've let you leave."

"Please don't worry about my feelings, Erika. That's really not important."

"Yes, it is!"

"I can see you're being your obstinate self!"

We both burst out laughing. The awkwardness between us had lifted and we were back to being old pals again. By the time we had left Dörfli behind, it was smooth sailing all the way to Davos. The resort town was alive with people strolling to restaurants, theaters and clubs, generating an atmosphere of pulsating nightlife. Erika maneuvered the car into a space at the *Kongresshaus* parking lot where the concert was held. Once seated, we still had ten minutes to spare before the performance began.

The first part of the program was dedicated to music composed by Johann Sebastian Bach. It commenced with the *First and Third Brandenburg Concertos* and then eased into one of his famous *Violin Concertos*. At intermission Erika made straight for the long line at the ladies room entrance. I was not as desperate and headed outdoors to have a cigarette. Standing amid the small cluster of smokers, I reflected on the pieces I had just heard and marveled at the genius of Bach.

In the second half we were treated to more lighthearted music by Wolfgang Amadeus Mozart, starting with the *Serenade in C major.* The lively and uplifting *Jupiter Symphony Number 41* made for a spectacular ending of the enjoyable evening.

I was humming Mozart's *Eine Kleine Nachtmusik* to myself as we walked to the car.

My friend commented, "You liked it?"

"Very much so. Thanks for taking me! I hope you were also able to relax and just enjoy the moment."

"Oh, I did. I tuned everything else out."

"Good for you!"

She nudged me, saying "Look who's walking toward us!"

Karl, with a young woman on his arm, ambled in our direction and said, "Hello there, Sis! I spotted you ladies from a distance. Enjoyed the concert?"

Without waiting for an answer he continued, "What are you up to now?" And turning to his date, "This is my sister, Erika Graff, and her friend Mrs. Huber." He paused, "And what is your name again?"

"Natasha," replied the young woman.

"That's right." He turned back to Erika and me, saying, "Meet Natasha. We're on our way to the piano bar around the corner. Care to join us?"

Erika glanced at me, and I gave a barely noticeable shake of the head.

She replied, "Thanks for the invitation, but we pass. We'd rather head home."

So we said good night and went our separate ways.

Chapter 24

On the drive back Erika remarked, "I'm glad you didn't want to take Karl up on his offer. I wasn't in the mood to have a drink with them either. Obviously his date was a one-night stand."

"It looked that way." Then I said, "You are his half sister, of course, but I was surprised he called you 'Sis.' Wouldn't it be more natural to just address you by your name?"

"He's always called me Sis, or big sister. When he was little, it amused him to have a sister old enough to be his mother. He got an even bigger kick out of his relationship to Stefan."

"Oh?"

She laughed and said, "Even though they were the same age, he insisted that Stefan call him Uncle Karl!"

"Did that bother Stefan?"

"Not in the least. They got along great. They were the best of friends," she replied.

Despite Erika's previous statement that she was "fine" now, I felt sure that reminiscing about her dead son's childhood must be painful.

So I changed the subject and asked, "How long was your dad married to his second wife?"

"Let me think," she said. "Karl was fourteen when Maria took off, so they must have been married about sixteen years."

Surprised, I asked, "You mean they didn't get a proper divorce? She just 'took off,' like you say?"

"Eventually there were divorce proceedings, but yes, one day out of the clear blue, she told Papa that she was 'running away' with a Spaniard, and a week later she was gone."

"Amazing!"

She said, "I wish she would have stuck it out. I really liked her."

"But obviously she and your dad had problems."

"No, they got along quite well."

"Erika, you're confusing me! Why would she run off if they got along?"

"Papa would say, 'It was the Gypsy in her.'"

I said, "Oh, I'm beginning to understand. Living at Talblick was too confining for her. But surely your father took her on trips and outings."

"Of course, but somehow it just wasn't enough."

"She needed more space?"

After a pause, my friend explained, "Okay. I'll tell you what my feelings are on the matter. At the time I thought about the reasons for her action a lot, but like I said, this is just my opinion. Neither Maria nor Papa ever talked to me about it."

She went on, "I found that they had been well suited to one another. Naturally they quarreled at times, but unlike Mamma, she was not afraid of him and stood her ground. Papa admired her for that. They did a lot of entertaining at Talblick, and she was an amusing hostess. She also helped out at the Sondereggli and seemed to enjoy the job. She was an excellent singer and dancer. Occasionally, Papa asked her to perform at the hotel or even at home. She was also a good mother. Papa was busy overseeing and running his hotels, but they spent his free time riding horses, playing tennis, skiing in winter and entertaining guests."

She continued, "All this kept her happy for a while, but as the years went by, she started getting antsy. Karl grew out of the little-boy stage and needed her less and less. As Papa got older, he wasn't too enthusiastic about traveling, unless it involved business trips.

"So one day when she helped out at the hotel, a wealthy guest from Spain came along, swept her off her feet, and took her away."

"Just like that!" I said.

She nodded.

After a pause I commented, "Your dad must have been upset."

"No kidding! He was devastated. It's hard to tell with Papa, but I believe he truly loved her. Most of all, his pride was hurt. A woman leaving Papa! Unthinkable!"

"How old was he at the time?"

"Sixty-one."

"And Maria is your age, so she was thirty-seven." I calculated.

"Correct."

Then I asked, "Did she end up marrying the Spaniard?"

"Yes, after the divorce from Papa was final."

"What about Karl? Did she take him along to Spain?"

"That's another story," Erika said, as she turned into the road leading up to Talblick. "They agreed that Karl would finish his education in Switzerland, so as not to disrupt his milieu. That worked out for a while, but after his schooling at age fifteen, he had to decide to either start an apprenticeship or to begin his studies for a higher education. Papa pressured him about enrolling in a hotel management school, but Karl wasn't interested and insisted on going to Spain to live with his mom. The long and short of it was that his new stepfather stuck Karl in an international boarding school, since the newlyweds were busy traveling all over the world at the time."

"I see."   And I inquired, "The boarding school was in Spain?"

"No, in Paris."

"So he got a good education?"

"Certainly. I believe he has a business degree. Karl is basically lazy, though. So far, he's been able to get by on his charm, it seems!"

"In what country did he finally make his home?"

"He's been all over the place," she replied. "He lived in Spain for a while, then moved to the South of France, then returned to Paris, and now he's back in Switzerland."

When we stopped in front of the mansion, I asked, "Did Maria stay married to her second husband?"

"Yes, but she's a widow now. Her husband died two years ago. The man came from an extremely wealthy family and left her a fortune."

Before getting out of the car, I remarked, "So Karl has nothing to worry about. He'll eventually inherit from his mom."

"If there's any money left by that time. Maria appears to be spending it like there's no tomorrow. She has traveled non-stop for the last two years!"

Chapter 25

Saturday morning I joined Erika on the veranda for breakfast. A few stubborn clouds tarried over the *Weissfluhjoch*, but the sun peeked through in a prelude to fair weather.

Looking at the panorama around us, I remarked, "We've got the best seats in the house!"

Erika said, "I love to eat out here, weather permitting."

"From what I glanced when we drove through Dörfli last night, the *Chilbi* is going to be huge."

"Oh, it's not just a regular carnival. They've combined it with an annual village-fest. Besides the rides, booths and stands, there'll be all sorts of contests and shows."

"Should be fun!"

When we had finished breakfast and sat with our second cups of coffee, she checked her watch and said, "I've got a couple of errands to run in Davos first. You can come along, or else I'll pick you up on my return."

"Why don't we just set a time and location to meet at the carnival?"

"Sure. You can ride down with someone else, if you prefer."

"That's not what I have in mind."

Perplexed, she asked, "And how are you planning to get to Dörfli?"

"On my own two feet!"

"Oh! Are you sure you want to walk?"

"Positive." And grinning, I added, "It's downhill, all the way!"

"So meet me in front of the big tent at 11:00 sharp," she ordered, picked up her plate and cup, and disappeared.

I lingered on the patio a while longer and then carried my dirty dishes to the kitchen as well. There was no sign of activity among the household members. Either everyone was sleeping in or kept busy elsewhere. I mounted the stairs to my room to freshen up, and then I took off for Dörfli.

On the way down, I noticed a narrow hiking trail crossing the road every so often. At one such intersection I contemplated taking the shortcut. I looked up to where the hiking path met the road, then crossed to the other side of the street to survey the down-slope where the trail continued. It appeared steep, going almost vertical with the mountainside. Since I was not equipped with proper footwear to tackle the path, I decided to stay on the main road.

At about the halfway mark to the village, a small red sports car raced up the hill. It came to an abrupt halt when level with me, and as I watched the driver-side window being rolled down, I realized it was Karl.

"Hey, Mrs. Huber! Where are you going at the crack of dawn?"

Glancing at my watch, I replied, "It's a quarter till ten and I'm headed for the *Chilbi*."

"Have a good time!"

"Will I see you there?"

"Maybe in the evening. Right now I'm going to bed."

I observed him more closely. It occurred to me that he probably hadn't seen a bed all night. Except for overnight stubble on his jaw, he looked none the worse for wear.

"Have a good snooze," I wished him.

He waved, stepped on the gas, and was gone in a flash.

Chapter 26

When I got to Dörfli, I had an entire hour to browse before meeting Erika. The fairgrounds extended over a generous part of the village. One section, which was normally an open field, was taken up by rides, stands and booths offering a variety of attractions like ring toss, darts, shooting gallery, et cetera. The other zone stretched over a couple of streets, which were cordoned off to traffic, where tables had been set up and merchants proffered anything from cooking spices to works of art. Connecting the two sections, a huge tent had been erected. This must be the entertainment tent, I gathered.

I first strolled around what in my mind I named the "Farmers Market." Astonishing, the items that were sold! An enthusiastic salesman tried to get me interested in purchasing a live parrot. The bird had addressed me, and anyone else that ambled by, with, "You're cute!" A beautifully ornate silk shawl caught my eye, but I resisted; too early in the day to be carrying merchandise around.

Next I ventured toward the amusement zone. There were kiddy rides and a few relaxing ones, like the Ferris wheel and merry-go-round, but most of the rides were clearly geared toward thrill-seekers. I spotted Lotti standing in line for a bumper-car ride. She was animated, obviously flirting with two boys also waiting to get on a bumper-car. That they might be "hicks" did not seem to bother her in the least. When I ambled by the *Himalaya* and the *Revolution*, I said to myself, I definitely want to ride these later.

Then I strolled back toward the big tent. Helga treaded my way, coming from the opposite direction in the company of a younger man, but as they came close, she averted her eyes and they passed by. I guessed she didn't feel like introducing her friend and so pretended she hadn't seen me. Could she perchance carry on an affair with the young man? I thought.

I came upon a bronze statue that I thought was mounted on a podium. The artwork portrayed a lovely lady dressed in a toga, with one arm gracefully extended and eyes that seemed fixed on something in the far distance. A small crowd had gathered, admiring the statue. I was wondering why one would find a Roman bronze in the middle of what normally was an open field. Then she moved! The lady shifted her position with a swift movement of her arms and head, and then stayed still, immobile again in another pose, not twitching a single muscle.

Before I moved on, I stepped over to her pedestal and said, "You're good! You fooled me for a minute."

The pantomime ignored me, staring straight ahead. I could not detect a single blink of her eyelids.

I walked on and got to a spot where people gathered in a circle around a clown. The buffoon was grabbing someone from the audience to help with his performance. I did not linger and continued on my course.

I was a few minutes early when I positioned myself at the tent entrance to wait for Erika. Folks were standing around nearby. Obviously, this seemed to be the people's appointed meeting place. I peeked inside the big tent. Nothing much was going on there yet. The rows of large rectangular tables were clad with red-and-white-checkered tablecloths, and the long benches pulled up beside them sat empty. Workers were busy with setting up props on the stage. In another hour or so, the place would be filled with people ready for lunch and entertainment, I mused.

As I turned toward the outdoors again, I heard a voice saying in English, "Hi there, Mrs. Huber!" and I found myself facing *Magic Fingers*.

"Well, hello, Laura! You're out to get the *Chilbi* experience, I see."

"I know *Chilbi* is a carnival, but this seems more like a County Fair."

I asked, "Are you alone?"

"I'm meeting my cousins in front of the tent. I hope this is the right one. I came upon a couple of smaller tents earlier."

"I'm sure this is it." And with a gesture encircling the crowd around us, I said, "The big tent seems to be the general meeting spot."

She had a large, red lip imprint on her cheek. Pointing to it, I remarked, "Someone got carried away!"

"Oh, did he leave a mark?" She took a tissue out of her purse and while wiping off the smudge explained, "That was from the clown. He pulled me into his circle and made the audience laugh at my expense. In the end, he rewarded me with a wet kiss on the cheek!"

She gestured at a bungalow nearby. The sign at the entrance read, *Preis Jassen,* and she said, "I know that *Preis* means 'prize', but what is *Jassen*?"

"*Jass* is a Swiss card game."

"There is gambling at a carnival?"

"I wouldn't call it gambling. It's more like a bridge tournament."

Then she asked enthusiastically, "Did you see the pantomime statue?"

"I sure did."

She went on, "Wasn't she the greatest? Her metallic makeup was applied to perfection, and she must have dipped that sheet she wears as a toga into metallic paint as well. I watched her for the longest time before I realized that she was a real person!"

"I was taken in too," I admitted.

While chatting, the young woman acted completely natural and carefree. I couldn't help but wondering if she was aware of what was going on around her at Talblick.

Since my curiosity was aroused, I asked, "Did Otto Sonderegger tell you he was making a new will?"

"He mentioned something to that effect," she replied.

"Do you know who the main beneficiary is?"

She raised an eyebrow and said, "I beg your pardon?"

"You are unaware that you'll inherit most of his estate?"

"Oh, that. Mr. Sonderegger hinted that he'd make me an heiress. I believe it when I see it," she said laughingly.

"You don't take his statement seriously?"

"Of course not."

I looked at her pensively and then proclaimed, "Laura Thompson, you hold uncommon wisdom!"

At that moment Erika arrived and I wished the court reporter a fun-filled day.

Chapter 27

Erika said, "Where to first?"

"Let's do some rides," I suggested.

"You've got to be joking!"

"What's wrong with rides?"

"We're too old, that's what."

I made a face at her. "Don't be a bore, Erika!"

She ignored the remark and said, "I hope you won't mind if Claude joins us a little later."

"Not at all. I'm dying to meet him."

We had arrived at the *Himalaya* ride, and I persuaded her to join me in the fun. She screamed a lot, especially while riding backward, but she clearly seemed to have a great time.

As we stepped off, she commented, "I hadn't done this in several decades!"

"See what you were missing!"

We boarded a couple of other rides and then came upon the *Revolution*. I urged her to join me on that particular thrilling enterprise.

She stated, "This is where I draw the line."

"But roller coasters are by far the most fun! You've got to do this one."

"No way!" she said. "This is no ordinary roller coaster. I refuse to ride anything that turns me upside down."

I assured her, "You'll get around the loop in a split second, and you won't even realize you're riding face down."

"Have you done it lately?"

My last experience on a similar ride was at Magic Mountain, California, and it dated back twenty years, but

I wasn't going to admit to that. So I said, "Not recently, but this ride has been around for a long time. I've been on it lots of times. As I recall, one gets a rush! Come on, don't be chicken."

I dragged her along, and as we sat down in the roller coaster car and the bars mechanically locked us in, she announced, "I'm going to have a heart attack!"

"What's wrong with your heart?"

"Nothing yet, but there will be in a second."

As soon as we started to move and picked up speed, I didn't hear a sound coming out of her mouth. She must be enjoying herself, I thought, and reveled in my own adventure of the moment. My reaction was a mixture of thrill and fear. When we walked away from the ride, I glanced at my friend. Her eyes were still big as saucers and there was a ghost-like pallor about her face.

When she had recuperated enough to speak, she said, "I'll never forgive you for this, Regula!"

We strolled on and came upon a food stand. I exclaimed, "Look, *Magenbrot*! And it comes in the pink paper bags I well remember. I just have to have some!"

Erika said, "It sure doesn't take much to get you excited. You must love the stuff."

"I haven't had *Magenbrot* in forty years. I forgot what it tastes like. All I know is that I used to devour it as a kid."

I made my purchase and then stuck one of the clumpy, brown cubes into my mouth. As I chewed, the memory of the unique, delicately spiced flavor came back in a flash.

"Delicious!" I proclaimed, holding the pink bag in front of her.

"Not for me. Thanks to you, I can't even look at food at the moment," she said accusingly.

I happily munched on my treats and remarked, "*Magenbrot* has such a distinctive taste, but I can't figure out what's in it."

"I can tell you the ingredients. I have a recipe."

"Really?"

"Sure," she said, "it's made with brown sugar, butter, eggs, coffee, flour, cocoa, ginger spice, cinnamon - - and what else? Let me think. Oh yes, rose water, Schnapps and red wine."

"No wonder it's so potent."

We sauntered on, and I remarked, "I saw Lotti earlier, but I didn't come across her parents."

"Oh, they just dropped Lotti off and went to Davos. I ran into them when doing my errands. They're in no mood for the carnival." And she continued, "Actually, everyone is anxious to get away, especially Norbert."

I said, "I'm surprised they're all staying put, then. I mean, your father made his announcement last night, so I would think everybody is free to leave."

"Wrong! Papa told Alex and Norbert this morning that he expects them to stay until he unveils whatever addition he's working on in the train room."

"That seems extreme, even for your dad."

She nodded. "I can't imagine what the big deal is about the new section he's currently building. He never made such a fuss over previous additions. Must be something extraordinary."

I smiled and declared, "I'm starting to get curious about what's under that plastic sheeting in his train kingdom! You'll have to write me all about it in the next e-mail."

"You can see for yourself. Papa said he'll finish the project by Monday or Tuesday."

"I'll be gone by then. I'm leaving for Bad Ragaz tomorrow morning."

"Shucks! And just as I was getting real comfortable having you around."

Then she said, "Let's head back to the big tent. Claude should be there soon."

I asked, "What kind of entertainment do they offer in the tent?"

"Right now, the attractions are mostly geared to family and kids. The program includes puppet shows, clowns, magic, and things like that. By evening and at dinnertime they might have singers or comedians. Then there'll be a band and dancing."

I noticed that the fairgrounds had become more crowded. I gathered that not only folks from Dörfli, Davos and the neighboring villages, but also people from the entire Kanton Graubünden had flocked to this spot.

We got to the *Jass* bungalow, and she said, "Just a minute, be right back," and disappeared inside.

When she joined me again, I inquired, "Are you interested in participating in the *Preis Jassen*?"

"Not me. I was checking up on Papa."

"Is he at the carnival?"

"Certainly. He's in there playing cards." And grinning, she added, "Should keep him busy for a few hours!"

"You won't have to worry that he'll see you together with your boyfriend."

"Precisely!"

Chapter 28

I wasn't sure what to make of Claude Boreau. He was casually dressed in jeans and a polo shirt when he swaggered toward us. There was nothing casual in the way he carried himself however, and the vain strut of a peacock came to mind. His dark hair, green eyes and straight narrow nose put him in a category of above average looks, a fact he seemed to be well aware of. Judging by the glow in Erika's eyes as they embraced, she appeared to be spellbound.

She introduced us, and he said, "*Enchanté, Madame Uber!*" without pronouncing the "H" in my name.

I replied in Swiss-German dialect, "Likewise, Mr. Boreau. Do you speak German?"

"Not if I can help it," he arrogantly countered in French.

So it became obvious that, while in this gentleman's company, we would speak French.

Then he said, "Erika told me about you," and, chuckling, he continued, "You're not my idea of a detective!"

"I'm sure you're not alone in that impression."

Then I asked, "What part of France are you from?"

"Oh, I'm Swiss, from Geneva."

We walked by a food stand and he said, "How about lunch?"

Erika agreed, "Yes, let's eat."

"You two go ahead. I'm full of *Magenbrot*. I'll just have a drink," I said.

We found an empty bench, and while they consumed their sandwiches, I turned to Erika's boyfriend and asked, "How do you like living in Davos?"

"I love it," he replied.

"What do you do?"

"I'm a chiropractor. I opened my practice here three years ago and it's doing well."

"What made you settle in Davos?"

"With all the sports activities going on in the town, there are plenty of patients with back injuries." And, grinning, he added, "Besides, one of my passions is skiing!"

"And another one is tennis?" I inquired.

"So Erika told you we met at the club. I wish she'd invite me to play at her house. I understand there is a perfectly good court up there."

Erika butted in, "You know how I feel about that, Claude. Don't rub it in, please."

We spent part of the afternoon browsing the market area, and I was happy to notice my silk shawl was still for sale. Then we ended up at the amusement zone once more. My friend made it clear that she was finished with rides, so we entertained ourselves with experiences like the haunted mansion, house of mirrors and the motorcycle cage. We also tried our luck at several game booths. We all won prizes: Claude did well popping balloons with darts, Erika had a winner by tossing rings over bottle-heads, and I shot a bull's eye into the target at the shooting gallery.

At dusk Claude bid us good-bye, and burdened with purchases and our trophies of stuffed animals, Erika and I walked to her car.

I said, "I had a great time!"

"Oh, we're not done yet. We'll just leave the parcels in the car and go back," she stated.

"Then what?"

"Helga has the day off, so there won't be any dinner at Talblick. I thought you might enjoy eating in the big tent, but we can drive to a restaurant in Davos, if you prefer."

"I'd love to eat in the entertainment tent," I assured her.

When we ambled back to the fair I asked, "Claude didn't want to dine with us?"

"We had an agreement that we would part before supper." And she seemed embarrassed as she explained, "More likely than not, Papa will show up in the big tent."

"I see."

She looked at me sideways and said, "You think I'm being silly, don't you?"

I shrugged my shoulders as I replied, "It is rather strange behavior, but hey, it's your life, Erika!"

Then she wanted to know, "How did you like Claude? Isn't he wonderful?"

I took a moment before I answered, "He seems to treat you well."

"But you don't like him?"

"I didn't say that."

"It's obvious that you don't, Regula!"

"That's not true. I just thought he was a little arrogant."

"Arrogant?" she said, dumbfounded. "What do you mean by that?"

"He's lived and worked here for three years and still insists conversing in French. I'm sure he has to communicate with his patients in Swiss-German. I bet his German is better than my French!"

"Don't be so hard on him. You know how French-speaking Swiss have difficulty with the pronunciation of our language."

I stated, "When in Rome do as the Romans do. I don't expect Swiss folks to speak to me in English."

"That's different," she said, "Swiss-German is your mother language."

Stubbornly, I shot back, "Nevertheless, I've lived in the United States so long that English flows easier from my lips."

After a pause she asked, "What else don't you like about Claude?"

"I'm not sure."

Irritated, she said, "What is that supposed to mean?"

"I just don't want you to get hurt, that's all."

"Get to the point. What's on your mind?"

I looked at her hard and then asked, "Are you going to tell him about your dad's new will?"

"I haven't thought about it. Why do you ask?"

"If I were you, I'd tell Claude that your dad's assets would eventually go to Laura Thompson. Then I'd sit back and see what happens."

She stood still and stared at me. Then she exploded, "You think he's a fortune hunter, don't you?"

"It has crossed my mind."

"You're dead wrong."

"I hope so."

"Besides," she declared, "Papa told me that no matter how he'd divide the rest of his estate, he'd always make sure I'd be well provided for, and that I'd inherit Talblick."

"I wouldn't mention that fact to Claude," I said.

"You are absurd!"

Chapter 29

We stood at the entrance inside the big tent. The place was crowded now, and we tried to locate a couple of empty seats. Then I spotted Otto Sonderegger waving to us from a table close to the stage at the other end of the tent, so we made our way over to him.

He professed, "It's about time some of you showed up! I can't hold the empty seats much longer."

As we sat down Erika said, "You can let other folks have the rest of the spaces. Alex and family are having supper in Davos, and I'm sure Norbert is not at the carnival. I don't know about Karl, but he might not want to sit with us anyway."

Within seconds, the seats were taken up by people anxiously looking for a place to sit.

I turned to the old man and asked, "How did you do at the *Preis Jassen*?"

"Not badly. I ended up in fourth place. How did you know I was at the *Jass* bungalow?"

Erika quickly replied, "Where else would you be, Papa?"

He chuckled and said, "I guess I'm predictable!"

The menu was pretty basic. We gave the waitress our orders of Bratwurst, Rösti, my favorite potato dish, and green salad. A teenage girl walked around selling raffle tickets. We each bought ten tickets at a franc apiece. The band members were busily setting up the stage with instruments, amplifiers and microphones. Then they did the usual - - testing, testing, one, two - - and started to play. I could tell right away that these were excellent musicians. They started off with a couple of country tunes. Nothing as patriotic as the national anthem, though. As the evening progressed, I was more and more impressed with the band. They played everything from big band, jazz, rock, pop and disco to ballroom dancing music, including some Latin rhythms. They even took requests from the audience.

Mr. Sonderegger seemed in excellent spirits that night. He appeared to enjoy listening to the tunes, moving his head in perfect timing to the beat. A fair amount of couples were flocking to the dance floor, and I watched their movements with interest.

We had long finished our meal and the time had advanced well into the night when I heard a voice behind us say, "Scoot over, Sis." I turned around and looked into Karl's grinning face. Then he squeezed onto the bench between Erika and me.

His father seemed pleased to see him and said, "So you finally decided to make an appearance!"

"Better late than never," Karl replied.

His dad remarked, "I was looking for you this morning."

"Why?"

"I want you to stay put until my new project in the train room is completed."

"Sure, I'll hang around for a while. I have no pressing business at the moment," Karl answered with a smirk.

The band started to play a Viennese waltz, and Mr. Sonderegger turned to Erika and said, "Come, girl, let's twirl around and show them how it's done!"

I observed father and daughter on the dance floor. They moved well together, and once more I was amazed at the agility of the old gentleman.

Karl smiled at me and said, "We'll go for it when they play something livelier, all right?"

"It's a deal," I replied. Then, looking down at my feet, I remarked, "These sandals are not the ideal footwear for the occasion!"

True to his word, when we heard the first few notes of a tune with a fast beat, the young man got up and with a mocking little bow pulled me to my feet and then followed me to the dance floor. He was an excellent dancer, and soon I was caught up in the rapid movements.

When the music came to a halt, he observed, "Sandals, or not, you've got perfect rhythm, Mrs. Huber! Let's stay on the floor and do another."

Slightly panting, I agreed, "All right, but let me catch my breath first!"

I was thankful that the next number turned out to be a leisurely foxtrot, and my heartbeat went back to normal. I surveyed the other couples dancing around us. All ages were represented: the young, the old and everyone in between.

On the way back to our table, Karl exclaimed, "Well, well! Look who's here!"

I followed the direction of his eyes and spotted Laura Thompson seated at a table way over on the opposite side of the tent. She sat between a young man and woman. I guessed the young people would be her cousins.

I said, "You've got eyes like a hawk! You picked her out clear across the place among all the strange faces!"

When we sat down again, the bandleader announced they would play one more tune before a short intermission.

At the first note, Karl jumped up, saying, "Lovely Miss Thompson, here I come!"

His father ordered, "You leave her alone, do you hear?"

Karl turned back to face him and, with an engaging smile, stated, "It's a free country, my dear Papa," and continued on his course.

It occurred to me that here was a son clearly not a bit afraid of his autocratic father and, what's more, tended to humor him. I watched Karl as he made his way across the place. Just when he got close to Laura's table, she and the young man got up and walked out to the floor. In order not to look like a total fool, Karl had no choice but to ask the other young lady at that table to dance.

Mr. Sonderegger had obviously followed his son's process as well. He tossed his head back and roared, "Ha ha ha! Serves him right!"

When I came out of the ladies room during intermission and was returning to our spot, I heard the winners of the raffle tickets announced. I was too late to catch what the first and second prizes amounted to, but the third was Appenzeller cheese. As I sat down next to Erika, the numbers of the third raffle were read off.

My friend glanced down at her ten tickets and mumbled, "95773. I'm close with 95770." Then she looked at me and said, "Hurry and get your tickets out."

I rummaged in my purse while the young man on the stage yelled into the microphone, "I repeat, number 95773! No taker? The owner of that ticket must have left already. I'll draw another number, then."

I raised my hand and yelled, "95773, right here!"

"Oh, I see a hand," said the announcer. "Yes, over there, the lady in red. Come on up and get your cheese!"

On stage, I was presented with an entire round, smelly Appenzeller cheese. The thing was about 25" in diameter and 7" high. As I carried my heavy treasure away, I wondered what on earth I should do with it. For the time being I placed it on top of our table.

Mr. Sonderegger eyed the cheese and remarked, "I'm curious as to how you'll smuggle this big guy on the plane?"

"I'll have to eat it all before I board," I joked back.

Karl nudged Erika and said, "Give me some leg-room, Sis. As soon as the music starts up again, I'll make a dash for my fair lady!"

He never got the chance, however, for when a number of people got to their feet and left during intermission, Laura and her cousins were among them.

When Erika drove us home, we had the back seat of her car loaded with purchases plus our winnings of stuffed animals, and a stinky cheese in the trunk.

I said, "The *Chilbi* was tons of fun! What a great last day for me!"

"Are you sure you don't want to stay a little longer?"

"It's time for me to move on," I said.

Chapter 30

On Sunday morning I found Helga in the kitchen stowing the dirty breakfast plates away in the dishwasher.

Unloading the giant cheese on the counter, I said, "Here's a present for you!"

She inspected the merchandise and then exclaimed, "A whole Appenzeller cheese! Why would you buy that for me?"

"I didn't. I won it last night, and I'm certainly not going to travel around with the smelly thing! I hope you can use it."

Clearly pleased, she said, "Of course I can. Thank you so much. I'll serve some for dessert tonight and divide the rest in sections. It will keep for a long time in the refrigerator."

Then I asked, "Do you know where Mr. Sonderegger is?"

"Out for a walk with Rex."

"I'll find him," I said, and bid the old housekeeper farewell.

I went along the old horse trail I had taken with my host on the first day of my visit, hoping he had chosen the same path. I was almost by the creek when I heard splashing, and then Rex came running toward me, wagging his tail. Just as I bent down to pet him, he shook himself furiously, getting me all wet. Then, wagging his tail rapidly again, the dog plopped down next to me. As expected, his master was not far behind.

He greeted me with, "Rex clearly likes you! He's treating you like an old friend." And he grunted, "I'm getting used to you myself!"

"Thank you!"

Then he asked, "Out for a stroll?"

"Actually, I was looking for you. I see you're on the way back to the mansion, so I'll keep you company."

"What's up?"

"I want to say good-bye and thank you for your kind hospitality."

"You can't leave yet. You have to stay until I unveil my new section."

I looked him in the eye and stated, "Sorry, but I'm leaving today. In half an hour, to be exact."

He suddenly burst out laughing and said, "You're not a bit afraid of me, Regula!"

"That might be because I'm not related to you," I countered.

We walked in silence for a while, and then I said, "You are playing a dangerous game."

"What do you mean?"

"I'm referring to your announcement about a new will."

"You think I'm bluffing, and you don't believe I'm going through with it?"

"It doesn't matter what I think. What your family makes of your statement is what's important."

"Ah yes," he said sarcastically, "my dear family!"

"Come now, Mr. Sonderegger! I know you don't disapprove of your offsprings as much as you pretend to."

"Erika is all right, and I like having her live with me. She is also useful to me on the rare occasions when I seek information from the Web. I am disappointed in my sons, no doubt."

"I can understand that, but you have to let go for your own peace of mind."

He said, "Oh, I gave up the idea of any of them taking over the hotel business decades ago, but it doesn't change my resentment." Then he continued, "I had great hope in my grandson. Now that remains an illusion as well."

Not for the first time since I'd come to Talblick, I felt sad for the old man. If only I could make him understand what is really important in the relationship with his family.

So I said, "How about if you take your sons just the way they are and enjoy them on their own merit?"

He looked like he was going to blow up at me but then apparently had a change of heart and remarked, "I'm going to miss our little chats!"

"Me too!"

"In answer to your question, I do like having my sons around. I especially enjoy Karl's company. He is a charlatan, no doubt. Plenty likable and charming, but a charlatan nonetheless." And he continued, "But I have every right to make my will and testament as I wish."

"Certainly."

Then he asked, "What did you mean earlier, when you said I was playing a dangerous game?"

"I think you know!"

He laughed and stated, "My sons wouldn't have the guts to harm me; none of them!" And he added, "Besides, Rex wouldn't let them."

I observed the German shepherd, happily trotting along next to his master, and commented, "I believe Rex would give his life for you."

Then, on a lighter note, I asked, "I'm just curious. I've noticed that some rooms are off limits to Rex, and others he's allowed to go into. For instance, he's welcome in the room where you dictate, but the massage room is forbidden to him."

"So?"

"I'm just wondering if there is rhyme and reason to your rules."

"You want to know which rooms he's allowed in and which ones not, and you also want to know why?"

"Yes."

"He's obviously not permitted in any of the guestrooms upstairs. I don't think Helga wants him in hers. He used to sleep in Erika's bedroom when I was away on trips. Nowadays, he hardly ever bothers to wander upstairs. He likes to be where I am."

"I've noticed," I said.

He went on, "At first I let him have the run of pretty much every room downstairs, except the kitchen and dining room, but I learned the hard way and had to forbid him the train room and what is now the massage room."

"Why?"

"There isn't much space for him to move around in the train room, and he was knocking things down, so I can't have him in there."

"What about the massage room?"

He grinned and said, "On the occasion of my first massage Rex attacked Weber. As Hans pounded my back, the dog thought I was in danger and jumped at him, going straight for the throat. I called him off before he caused any damage, but it frightened the man to death."

Then I asked, "Where does Rex sleep?"

"On the rug next to my bed," he answered.

At that point we had arrived at the mansion. I thanked my host once more, fetched my packed suitcase, and then Erika drove me to the Dörfli train station.

Chapter 31

My friends dropped me off at the Bad Ragaz station on Tuesday morning. I bought a ticket and was waiting to board the next train to Zurich. We had experienced thunderstorms with heavy rain throughout most of Monday, so I had been content to stay indoors at my friends' home in Bad Ragaz. The visit with them had been enjoyable, but now I was ready to head for the hometown of my childhood. I was looking forward to spending some quality time with my sister, as well as strolling through Old Town Zurich. I purposely neglected calling my sister about the planned arrival that day, as I didn't want to bother her with having to pick me up. I intended to just take the tram and surprise her.

Surveying the sky, I was happy to observe that the storm clouds had passed and to be allowed to bask in another pleasant summer's day. I imagined that my brother-in-law would take us out to dinner someplace in Old Town that evening. Then we'd amble through the Niederdorf to Bellevue Square, over the bridge and down the Limmatquai. I remembered clearly what an impressive picture Zurich painted at night, with the steeples of the Grossmünster and Fraumünster, as well as other old buildings, lit up along the river Limmat.

The ringing of the phone in my purse startled me out of my reverie.

Surprised that my husband would call me at this time of day, I said, "Hi, Peter. What's up?"

"No. It's Erika."

"Erika! How did you get this number?"

"From your sister," she said, "but never mind that. Where are you?"

"At the Bad Ragaz station. I'm boarding a train to Zurich in a couple of minutes," I replied.

I heard the urgency in her voice, as she pleaded, "Don't get on the train. You've got to come back. Please stay put. I'll come get you."

Astonished, I asked, "You want me to come back to Talblick?"

"Yes, please!"

"What happened?"

"Papa is ...dead!"

The train roared into the station and I couldn't hear a thing. I waited until the noise subsided, and then said, "I must have misunderstood. I thought I heard you say that your father was dead."

"You heard correctly."

"Oh, Erika! I am so sorry!" And after a pause I added, "He seemed so healthy. How did he die?"

There was pain in her voice as she explained, "He drowned in the miniature lake of his train room."

I pictured the small pool of water in my mind. It had appeared about one foot deep, one-and-a-half at most. Erika's words made no sense.

I said, "But the mini lake is shallow! How could he have drowned in it?"

When she didn't answer, I urged, "How did it happen?"

"At first we thought it was an accident, but now it looks like he was murdered."

"Oh no! When was he killed?"

"Yesterday." And she begged, "Regula, I need your help! You have to come back and solve this."

I watched my train to Zurich roll out of the station and said, "Surely you called the police!"

"Of course. They've already questioned us all." Then she said, "I'm afraid they suspect Norbert. You've got to help him, I beg you."

"What makes you think the authorities suspect Norbert?"

She was near hysterics when she replied, "They wanted the address of where the auction is held in Basel. I'm sure they're on their way to arrest him, as we speak. It looks bad for Norbert, but I know he wouldn't hurt a fly. Please come back and find out what happened to Papa."

"The police might not want me to interfere."

"Probably not, but they can't prevent me from hiring you."

"True, but - -"

"Do it for me. I'm desperate!"

After a long pause, I finally said, "All right. I'm going to exchange my train ticket to Zurich for one taking me back to Dörfli."

"Don't bother. You'd have to change trains in Landquart again. It'll be a lot faster by car. Just stay put and I'll pick you up shortly," she said and hung up.

Chapter 32

Neither of us spoke for the first few miles of the drive. The pallor in Erika's face and the dark circles under her eyes illustrated that she'd had a sleepless night. However, she seemed to have herself under control. I was thinking back to my last walk with Mr. Sonderegger only two days earlier. The forceful personality of the old man lingered in my mind.

I broke the silence and said, "Okay, Erika. Tell me exactly what happened."

"I don't know. As I told you, we first thought it was an accident, but the police are treating it as a homicide."

"Tell me what you do know."

She shuddered and then said, "It was horrible! I can't get the picture out of my mind. Papa's head was submerged in the miniature lake, and Rex hovered next to him, not letting anyone near. The vet had to shoot the dog with a tranquilizing gun before anyone could get to Papa."

I asked, "So Rex was in the train room with your dad?"

"I guess he ran in as soon as the door was opened."

"Who found him?"

"Rita Schmied, the cleaning lady."

"At what time?"

"Around 3:00 in the afternoon."

"Was the entire family present?"

"Yes," she replied, "they hung around, but they were anxious to leave."

"I'll have to question them all, as well as the staff."

"I understand." Then she said, "Do whatever it takes to find out who killed Papa."

After a pause I said, "You told me the police were going to interrogate Norbert in Basel, so I assume he is no longer at the house?"

"He left last night," she answered.

"Is everyone else still there?"

"Yes, they are."

Then I asked, "When did you see your father last alive?"

"Yesterday at lunch, and he was in a rotten mood. He picked a fight with us all."

"Why do you think the police suspect Norbert? You mentioned that they had questioned everyone. I mean, if they suspect him, why would they let him leave?"

"Someone must have told the police what he said at lunch."

"Oh?"

She did not explain, but burst out, "It looks bad for Norbert, but I know he didn't do it."

I glanced over at my friend. She had an intent grip on the steering wheel, and she never averted her eyes from the road.

I ordered, "Erika, tell me exactly what was said during lunch. I also need to know who was present. Tell me every detail of the conversation. Leave nothing out."

She took a deep breath and then stated, "We were having lunch when Papa burst in on us and - -"

"At what time was that?"

"It must have been around noon."

"Who was having lunch?"

"Alex, Mirella, Lotti, Norbert and me. As I said, Papa came in and amused himself by nagging everyone. Then - -"

"Was this in the dining room?"

"No, we were eating at the kitchen counter."

"Sorry for interrupting again," I said, "but you need to be precise. It might be important."

She went on, "Okay - - let's see. Papa never sat down to have lunch, by the way. He apparently just came to tell us a thing or two and started with me by asking, 'Where did you spend the night?' I was taken off guard and didn't answer. Then he told me that he had wanted me to do some research on the Internet for him, and that he came to look for me early that morning. He said that he couldn't find me in my room or office and that my bed didn't look like it had been slept in, so he checked the garage and noticed that my car was gone. At that point I was mad and shot back, 'At my age I certainly don't have to check with you before I decide to spend the night elsewhere.'

"Then he harped on Lotti, saying, 'Your eye-shadow is applied so heavily, I'm surprised your lids don't stay permanently shut from the weight!' Lotti murmured something like, 'What would you know about eye-makeup, you old fart,' but I don't think Papa heard her. Next he mocked Norbert by remarking, 'Don't look so frustrated. You might still make it to your auction on time! And if not, I'm sure people can manage without your fussiness.'"

She continued, "He then turned on Alex and said, 'As for you, I'm sure the world finances won't collapse without your meddling.' After he was done disapproving of everyone, he told us that he was going to finish the project in the train room that afternoon, but first he would have a short session with *Magic Fingers*. Papa's last words as he left the kitchen were, 'So all of you, stick around for the unveiling!'

"As soon as Papa was out of earshot, Mirella said angrily, 'He's toying with us, of course. Rubbing it in that he'll have a session with the Thompson woman. Someone ought to put a stop to him.' Alex calmed her down and reminded her that at least it appeared that Papa's project was going to be completed soon, and then they could all go home."

Erika's voice got a little shaky as she went on, "Norbert suddenly exploded, 'Who the hell cares about his idiotic project. I'd love to see Papa's precious trains crash on him, or better yet, have him drown in his silly mini lake!' At the moment of Norbert's outburst, Karl had joined us, and he teased, 'Well, well, what do you know! The gentle Norbert is harboring violent thoughts!'"

We were driving along the main road of Davos when my friend's testimony ended, and then neither of us spoke. I mulled over what she had told me. I could picture that lunch scene at Talblick vividly, as if I had been a witness to it.

When we got close to Dörfli, Erika remarked, "You see now why I think Norbert is in trouble."

I replied, "Harboring violent thoughts, to use Karl's words, is a far cry from taking violent action."

"Oh, Regula! I'm so glad you see it that way." And she added, "You'll find out what really happened to Papa, won't you?"

"I'll try."

We were driving around the last few bends before getting to the estate when I said cheerfully, "So you spent Sunday night at Claude's house, huh?"

Despite the sad occasion, I got a smile out of her as she said, "My first overnighter at his place, and leave it to Papa to get wise to it!" And she continued, "I had meant to leave Claude's apartment around 2:00 in the morning but couldn't get my car started. So we decided I might as well stay the entire night and worry about the car later.

We had it towed to a repair shop first thing in the morning, and then Claude drove me home."

"The car seems to be running fine now. When did you get it back?"

The expression on her face got grave again as she replied, "I had forgotten all about it after what happened yesterday afternoon. The mechanic dropped my car by in the midst of all the commotion. Of course, the man saw the police and coroner vehicles parked in front of the house. The news must have spread all over Dörfli by now."

When she let me out in front of the mansion, I pointed to a car parked near the entrance, saying, "Whose is that?"

"That belongs to Ernst Knupp of the police," she answered.

Chapter 33

I had just finished unpacking my bag and stowing my things in the guest room once more when Erika came to get me, saying, "Ernst Knupp wants to question you when you're ready."

"I'm ready now," I replied, grabbed my purse and followed her down the stairs.

She stopped in front of a door adjacent to her late father's bedroom and said, "He's using Papa's office, go right in."

The man who sat behind the desk was wearing a white dress-shirt and a blue-and-gold-striped tie. His navy blazer hung over the back of the chair. He might have been in his early forties and had a square, clean-shaven face. He wore his brown hair cut short with a few strands stubbornly sticking straight up on top of his head. The look reminded me of Alfalfa in *The Little Rascals*. He got up, and I felt a pair of keen blue eyes scrutinizing me.

He extended his hand and introduced himself, "Ernst Knupp from the *Kriminal Abteilung* of the *Kantonspolizei Graubünden* in charge of this case." And pointing to the chair in front of the desk he said, "Have a seat, Mrs. Huber."

As we both sat down, I asked, "How do I address you, Detective or *Postenchef*?"

"*Herr* Knupp will do. We don't make a point about titles here."

Then he said, "I understand you are visiting from the United States. Can I see your passport, please?"

I was prepared. I reached into my purse and handed it to him together with my business card. He opened the passport, studying it at length.

Then he looked at me and stated, "Place of birth: Switzerland. Yet you travel with an American Passport. How long have you lived in the United States?"

"A lifetime. I moved there when I was twenty."

Not without humor he remarked, "You needed a broader horizon!"

Then he paid attention to my business card and said, "Mrs. Graff informed me that she hired you to investigate her father's murder, and I cannot prevent her from doing so. However, I'd like to point out that you have no jurisdiction in this country, let alone in this Kanton, Detective R.A. Huber."

I smiled and replied, "I have no official jurisdiction anywhere in the States either. I'm a *private* investigator."

He nodded and then said, "You can do your private investigating as long as it doesn't interfere with our department's progress in the case."

"I appreciate that, Herr Knupp."

He continued, "Do you have any other identification on you?"

"Yes, my California driver's license," and I got my wallet out.

He raised his hand in protest and said, "You don't have to show it. I just want to make sure that you're not left without I.D., since I need to borrow your passport for a day or two."

"Go ahead and take it. I'm not likely to travel in the next couple of days!" And I added, "You may keep my card."

"Thank you."

He got down to business and said, "Now then, first things first. At this time I am continuing *my* investigation by questioning *you*." So the formalities of my full name, age, marital status, home address and phone number, et cetera, were established.

Then he asked, "I understand you were a guest in this house for a few days?"

"That is correct."

"Tell me exactly when you arrived and when you left."

"I got here last Wednesday afternoon and left Sunday morning. Actually, I spent Wednesday night at Hotel Sondereggli in Davos and then stayed in this house starting Thursday at Otto Sonderegger's invitation."

"I was under the impression that you are Mrs. Graff's friend, so wasn't it she that invited you?"

I replied, "I've been Erika's friend since childhood, but of course I've always known her father as well."

"I see." And he continued, "What time did you leave on Sunday?"

"I caught the 10:14 train out of Dörfli that morning. My friend drove me to the station around 10:00."

Mr. Knupp questioned me further, "Where did you spend your time between Sunday morning at 10:00 and now?"

I answered, "I took the train from Dörfli to Bad Ragaz, with a changeover in Landquart. I stayed with friends in Bad Ragaz. From there, I had planned to travel back to Zurich this morning when Erika called and told me about her father."

"Please give me your Bad Ragaz friends' address and phone number. We need to verify your whereabouts."

I complied. Then I rummaged in my bag and pulled out my cancelled train ticket from Dörfli to Bad Ragaz, saying, "Here is proof I was on the train last Sunday."

He surveyed the ticket, then raised an eyebrow and said, "My experience has been that the train attendant collects the ticket on the last stretch of the journey."

"I begged him to let me keep it."

He said sarcastically, "To have it conveniently ready in case you would need an alibi?"

I calmly replied, "My five-year old grandson collects all kinds of tickets. So far I've accumulated the following tickets on my trip: Paddlewheel-ship on lake Zurich, chairlift up a mountainside in Merano, park-house toll in Aix-les-Bains, train from Zurich to Davos, Bach and Mozart concert, several carnival rides, and the one I just showed you."

"I get the picture."

After a pause, he questioned, "Have you formed an opinion of who the murderer might be?"

Perplexed I replied, "Mr. Knupp, I just got here!"

"I meant from what you previously observed as a guest in this house."

"At that time I had no idea I'd have to look for a murder suspect."

He eyed me intently and then said, "So you didn't detect any ill feelings, quarrels or disagreements among the family?"

I shrugged and said, "There is a certain amount of disagreements in most families."

"I'm thinking of something specific."

"Really?"

"Don't act ignorant, Mrs. Huber. I understand you were present when the victim announced that he was changing his will and leaving most of his money to an outsider!"

"You are well informed," I remarked.

"Tell me what you thought of the matter."

"It was none of my business."

His voice held command when he insisted, "I want to know what you thought at the time. Did you feel that Otto Sonderegger was bluffing, or was your intuition that he was making a new will in favor of Laura Thompson?"

I waited a moment before I answered, "At the time I felt Mr. Sonderegger was just amusing himself by threatening his sons with making that new will. Then later, I wasn't so sure anymore."

"What do you mean by 'later'?"

"I had a conversation with Mr. Sonderegger shortly before I left for Bad Ragaz. The subject of his new will came up. As I said, at that point I wasn't sure what to think about the matter. The old gentleman wasn't easy to read."

"I see."

"Surely, as police officer in charge of the case, you'll have no problem in getting information from Otto Sonderegger's estate lawyer about his will."

"We're looking into that, of course. I just wanted your personal impression."

Then he said, "Thank you, Mrs. Huber. That's it for the moment. I might question you further at a later time."

As I got to my feet I inquired, "May I ask you a question?"

"Certainly."

"How was Otto Sonderegger killed?"

"He was hit over the head with a blunt instrument, rendering him unconscious. Then he was drowned in 30 centimeters of water," he replied. I silently calculated and thought, that's roughly one foot.

Then I asked, "May I have a look at the murder scene?"

"Surely. We're done in there." And standing up, he added, "I'll come with you."

Chapter 34

There was chaos awaiting us in the train room. Apparently, trains had collided with one another and lay derailed. Some of them had obviously crashed into miniature stations, houses, crossing gates, tunnels and so forth before they came to a halt and lay on their sides or upside down. I glanced at the lake and shivered. Then I looked over to where the plastic sheeting had covered the new addition two days before and saw nothing but rubble. The freshly papier-mâchéd area had collapsed and lay in shambles with a gaping hole at its center. We would never find out what Otto Sonderegger's new project was all about now.

I asked, "Was the waterfall still flowing into the lake when you came to the scene?"

Mr. Knupp replied, "Yes, we found it intact. A pump recycling the water activated it. We turned the pump off after we were through in here."

"What caused the havoc? Was Otto Sonderegger putting up a fight?"

"Not at all. I doubt he knew what hit him. He had an extensive wound on the back of his head. The control device apparently had slipped out of his hands when he was struck and then drowned. So the trains had a free run for a while before they finally crashed and derailed."

I was puzzled and questioned, "Surely the collision of trains could not have caused that entire area next to the lake to cave in?"

"The victim's left arm and shoulder had crashed into that part of the display when his head was pushed into the lake, causing the entire area to collapse and be totally destroyed."

I couldn't help but shiver again. Then I said, "I heard that Rex had to be tranquilized before anyone could get near Mr. Sonderegger."

"That's right. When Mrs. Graff called us, she mentioned that the dog was hovering near the victim, growling at anyone trying to approach. We've had to deal with dogs protecting their masters before and knew what to expect. So I called the vet who arrived shortly after we did."

"Could Otto Sonderegger have been helped if someone had gotten past Rex right away?"

"Most unlikely. We arrived at the scene twelve minutes after we received the call, and he'd already been dead approximately half an hour at that time."

I glanced at the tool shelf by the window and, pointing to it, stated, "There is something missing here. Last time I was in this room, I saw a hammer on that shelf."

"You are observant, Mrs. Huber! We took the hammer to our lab for analysis."

"Was it the weapon used to knock Sonderegger unconscious before drowning him?"

"Possibly."

He looked at his watch and said, "I have to get going."

"I think I've seen enough," I murmured and followed him to the door. Just before reaching it I turned around and surveyed the room once more.

I shook my head and remarked, "You should have seen the ingenious layout of this place when it was up and running. It was splendid!"

"I'm impressed with the site even as it is now," he replied.

Chapter 35

In the afternoon I borrowed Erika's car and drove to Dörfli equipped with directions to Rita Schmied's house. After taking the first few curves, I suddenly thought, please God, prevent any cars from coming up the road in the next few minutes!

I found the modest home on a side street off the main road and pulled into a small dirt lot next to the house. When I got out of the car, the front door opened and Mrs. Schmied came to greet me. She was not wearing her scarf any longer.

I said, "Your perm looks good!"

"Thank you."

Pointing at the car I asked, "May I leave it here?"

"Of course." Then she said, "Like I told you when you called, I wouldn't have minded in the least driving up to the mansion."

We stepped over her threshold, and I said, "I thought it might be easier for you to talk to me on your own turf. Besides, we probably have more privacy here."

"That's true. My husband is at work, so we have the place to ourselves."

She led me to a cozy living room, motioned me into an upholstered chair and asked, "How about some coffee?"

I just had consumed lunch and was fully satisfied, but I didn't want to offend her. So I said, "I'd love some."

She disappeared into the kitchen, and I looked around at an unpretentious, spotless room containing furniture polished to a sheen. Photos of a chubby baby girl at various stages of her development were displayed, some hanging on the walls, others standing on the mantel and bookshelf. Mrs. Schmied returned carrying a tray loaded with a pot of coffee, two cups with saucers and a dish stacked with cookies.

"You shouldn't have gone to such trouble," I said.

"No trouble at all!"

I gestured to the pictures and asked, "Your grandchild?"

"Yes, our first," she answered proudly.

"We have three. Grandkids are precious, aren't they?"

I forced myself to sample a cookie. It was stale and bone dry, but the coffee was freshly brewed and tasted excellent. Then I felt it was time to get to the point.

I began, "As you know, I'm looking into yesterday's tragedy."

Her face became grave as she said, "Yes, ma'am."

"You discovered Mr. Sonderegger's body. Correct?"

She nodded.

"Tell me exactly how that came about."

She shuddered. "It was horrible! I'll never forget it."

"Did you come upon the scene as you were about to clean the train room?"

"Oh no," she said, "Mr. Sonderegger never allowed me to touch anything in that room. He insisted on dusting and vacuuming it himself, but I doubt he ever really gave the place a good cleaning."

"Please tell me how and at what time you found your employer. I need to know every detail."

"I don't know what time it was exactly. Must have been close to 3:00 in the afternoon. I had finally gotten around to cleaning Mr. Sonderegger's office, since he wouldn't let me in earlier. Like I said, I was vacuuming the office, and when I turned the vacuum cleaner off to move some furniture around, I heard Rex barking. I didn't pay much attention to it at first. I thought Rex just didn't like the storm. I turned the machine back on and continued my vacuuming. When I finished, Rex was still barking, so I went out to the corridor to see what was going on. I found the dog in front of the train room barking like mad and scratching at the door. I had never seen him this frantic. He's a well-trained animal. I figured something must be wrong and knocked, and getting no response, I went in."

She took a deep breath before she continued, "Trains lay derailed and part of the display had collapsed. Amid the mess there was Mr. Sonderegger bent down with his head in the lake. Rex ran past me, came to a stop by his master, gave a couple of howls, and then stood guard next to him. At first I was in shock, and then I screamed and ran out of the room."

She paused before she went on, "I think I was still screaming when the young American woman came toward me in the hallway and wanted to know what the commotion was about. I just pointed to the train room. I couldn't bring myself to go back there again."

"That's understandable." And I asked, "Did you run into anyone else besides Laura Thompson?"

"No, but I pulled myself together and went upstairs to tell Mrs. Graff that her father had met with a terrible accident. Then I came down again and told Miss Hodler. I never went back to the train room, but later I found out that Rex wouldn't let anyone near Mr. Sonderegger, not even Mrs. Graff. The vet had to tranquilize the animal."

"I heard about that," I commented.

With finality in her voice the cleaning lady stated, "That's all I know. When the police questioned me, I told them everything I just told you."

I reflected on her story. There was no point in going over the murder scene again; I could picture that well enough. So I said, "You mentioned that you couldn't clean Mr. Sonderegger's office earlier. Why was that?"

She explained, "I usually clean his bedroom, bathroom and office all in a row, since they are connected, but yesterday morning - -"

"What do you mean by 'connected'?"

"His bedroom has a connecting door to the bathroom on one side and to the office on the other."

"I see. Please continue."

"So yesterday morning while cleaning Mr. Sonderegger's bedroom, I heard him talking to someone in the office. The connecting door was closed, and at first I thought he was talking to Rex. Then I realized another person was there. I knocked and asked if I might enter to clean the room. He yelled that he was busy and not to be disturbed. So I waited with getting to his office until later."

"I understand now. Do you know who he was talking to?"

"No, I don't."

"Did you hear anything of the conversation?"

Vexed, she replied, "I don't listen at doors!"

I quickly said, "Oh, I'm not suggesting that you had eavesdropped. Mr. Sonderegger had a strong voice, and I thought you might inadvertently have caught something he said."

She seemed reassured that I didn't think badly of her and remarked, "Come to think of it, I did hear a bit of the conversation, but it didn't make sense to me."

"Of course not, but tell me anyway."

"Well, Mr. Sonderegger sounded mad and talked about deception of some kind."

"This might be important. Try to remember his exact words."

She took a moment to think, and then recalled, "He said something like, 'You went behind my back and deceived me.' Then the person made a reply, but talked too low for me to hear. Whoever it was talked for some time, but I couldn't make out what was said. The dog was definitely in the office too, because I heard Mr. Sonderegger tell him '*Platz*, Rex,' once, while the other person was talking."

I asked, "And that was all you gathered from the discussion?"

"I think so." Then she reconsidered and added, "He said something that had to do with law."

"Who said? Mr. Sonderegger?"

"Yes. I never could make out what the other person talked about."

"Try to remember what Mr. Sonderegger mentioned about law."

After a pause she recalled, "I think I heard him say, 'You have no legal right whatsoever.'"

Then I asked, "The other voice you heard, was it male or female?"

"I don't know," she answered.

"Surely you had formed an impression whether the voice you heard was male or female, even if it wasn't clear."

"At the time I thought it was a woman's voice, but later, when I saw the stranger, I figured the voice must have been his."

"Tell me about the stranger, Mrs. Schmied."

"There isn't much to tell. A little later, when I was coming out of the family room into the hallway, I noticed a stranger walking down the corridor toward the entrance-hall. I figured the man came from Mr. Sonderegger's office and was on his way out."

"Did you get a good look at him?"

"No. I only saw him from the back."

"Let me picture this clearly in my mind. You were standing in the hallway near the family room when you noticed a man coming out of Mr. Sonderegger's office. Right?"

"Yes, but I didn't actually see him come out of the office. He was already past the office door when I saw him. I assumed he came out of there. Where else would he have been coming from?"

I said, "The family room is at the end of the hallway, which is a distance away from where this man had apparently been walking along the corridor. How can you be sure he was a stranger and not one of the family guests? You didn't see his face."

She stubbornly insisted, "I just know I had never seen that man before in my life."

I changed the subject and asked, "At what time did you clean Mr. Sonderegger's bedroom?"

"Around 9:00 in the morning."

"And when you vacuumed his office it was near 3:00 in the afternoon?"

"That's right."

"Was the reason you waited so long to get back to cleaning his office because you were under the impression he stayed there for hours?"

"Not at all. I saw him roaming around."

"Meaning?"

"I noticed him leaving through the sliding-glass door going out to the veranda, obviously taking Rex for a walk while it had stopped raining for a bit. Then later Rex was sitting by the door while his master was getting a massage. At noon I was going to have a bite to eat, but some of the family was having lunch in the kitchen, and I decided to have my meal later. On my way out I almost collided with my employer when he apparently also headed for the kitchen. I didn't see him anymore after that, but of course I knew he was in the train room later in the afternoon, because Rex was sitting by the door."

Then she said, "To answer your question, I had forgotten about not having cleaned the office yet. I was just thinking that all I had left to do was to scrub the other two bathrooms downstairs when I remembered. So I cleaned the office first."

With a sad expression on her face, she continued, "Needless to say, after what happened next, I never got around to those bathrooms."

We sat quietly for some time. Obviously the cleaning lady was consumed with the tragedy she had witnessed. The image of the lake and the collapsed section in the train room came to my mind as well.

I finally said, "Moving around while doing your job yesterday, you must have a pretty good idea where everyone was before and around 3:00."

With a sudden spark of humor she replied, "Well, I can tell you one thing, nobody was outdoors! When I was cleaning the office, the lightning was so close that the house literally shook with each blast of thunder. The rain came down in buckets too."

I nodded. "It was an enormous storm. I experienced it while staying in Bad Ragaz."

She got serious again and continued, "Let me see. I saw the Alex Sonderegger family play a board game in the family room a while earlier. I think Miss Hodler was in the kitchen. The American was working on her computer. Hans Weber was doing laundry, but he might have finished and left by then. Mrs. Graff was in her office upstairs when I went to tell her about what happened. I don't know about Norbert and Karl Sonderegger. I'd guess they were in their rooms upstairs."

"You really keep your eyes open," I said, approvingly. She beamed at me.

I couldn't think of any more questions to ask her. I thanked the lady for the coffee and cookies and got up to leave.

Chapter 36

Back at the mansion, I found Erika, Alex and Karl in the living room obviously engaged in serious discussion. They labored over address book and notepaper, clearly making lists of people to contact. I didn't want to intrude, so I just left the car key on the credenza. Then I went up to my room to change into sneakers with the idea of taking Rex for a walk. I had not seen the dog at all since my return to Talblick. Perhaps he was outside waiting for someone to take him for a stroll. When I got to the veranda, there was no sight of the dog, but I spotted Lotti stretched out on the hammock. I walked over, and as I stood by it looking down on her, I noticed that she had been crying.

I said, "It's good to grieve. Let it all out. You'll feel better afterwards."

She gave me a look like a wounded animal and exclaimed, "You don't understand!"

"Try me."

She didn't respond, but I knew she needed to pour her heart out. So I waited and stood next to the distressed teen for quite some time. She seemed oblivious, as if she had forgotten I was there.

Suddenly she burst out, "I was nasty to Opa ever since we got here. I called him an old fart yesterday. Then he got killed and I can't take it back."

"Sure you can," I said.

She stared. Then a glimmer of hope showed in her big brown eyes as she asked, "You think he can see me from wherever he is?"

"Possibly. Besides, from what I gathered about your grandpa's personality, he might have secretly gotten a kick out of your spunk when you blurted out the disrespectful remark." Then I said, "I'm sure you had good times with your grandfather. Remember those."

After a pause she shared, "He was an interfering tyrant, but I loved him." She smiled as she recalled, "He taught me how to ride. When I was little, he bought me a pony. Then later, he let me ride all his horses. My favorite was a beautiful gray mare named Bella.

"I especially enjoyed the winter-sport vacations with him. One day last season he challenged me to a race, him on skis and me on the snowboard." She grimaced as she went on, "You'd think it would be easy to outrace such an old man, but I didn't stand a chance!"

"Cherish those moments with your grandfather. In time, the quarrels will fade from your memory."

"I hope so."

Then I said, "Do you know why I came back to Talblick?"

"Yes. Aunt Erika told us," she replied.

"I need to ask you about yesterday."

"Go ahead. It can't be worse than the policeman's questioning."

"What did you do yesterday?"

"You want to know about my whole day?"

"Let's say, starting at noon."

"We had lunch around 12:00. Opa came into the kitchen while we were eating and told us he was going to finish his project in the afternoon. That's when I was rude to him. After he left, Uncle Norbert said something much worse, but I don't want to repeat it."

"I know what he said."

"Who told you?"

"Your Aunt Erika."

"Oh! I didn't think she'd rat on him."

I replied, "She wasn't ratting. You have to understand, I need to know every detail of conversations and events in order to investigate."

"I guess so." Then she said, "At the time Uncle Norbert made the remark, I didn't think it was all that bad. I thought it was funny. Later, when it turned out Opa didn't have an accident but somebody killed him, it was creepy to know it happened just the way Uncle Norbert said."

I asked, "So what did you do after lunch?"

"There wasn't much to do, with the rain and all. I went up to my room and called my friend who had just come back from Venice. She told me all about the cute local boy she met. She must have exaggerated, though. I don't think her Italian is good enough to have grasped all the stuff he supposedly had said to her."

I smiled and commented, "Probably romantic wishful thinking on your friend's part."

She continued, "Later, Daddy came to see me and suggested we play games in the family room. So I followed him downstairs."

"What time was that?"

"I don't know. Maybe 1:30 or 2:00, or even later."

She went on, "When we got to the family room, Mom was already there rummaging through the games. There is a shelf with cards, chess, backgammon and all sorts of board games. She said she had asked Uncle Norbert to come play cards with us, but he was packing so he'd be ready to leave as soon as the train room thing was over with. Dad only likes to play cards when there are four people, so we can play partners. With only the three of us, we ended up playing Monopoly."

I exclaimed, "Monopoly! We used to play Monopoly when I was a kid!"

"It's pretty lame," she said, "but better than the other choices we had." And she kept going, "After we were well into the game, the storm got close. You couldn't even count to two between lightning and thunder. I've had a fear of thunderstorms ever since I was caught in one while hiking in the mountains. So yesterday I got pretty scared. Mom said I should just tune it out and concentrate on playing the game. How could I tune out the ear-piercing blasts shaking me in my chair, I ask you?"

"Really frightening, huh?"

She nodded.

Then she continued, "We heard Rex bark, and Daddy said, 'Rex doesn't like the storm either.' We heard the barking and howling again after the sound of thunder stopped. Then someone screamed and Dad opened the family room door. Mom and I followed him into the hallway where we saw the cleaning woman running away in the other direction, screaming at the top of her lungs. She ran past Laura Thompson, who was headed toward us. I went after my parents, walking down the hallway. The door to the train room was open, and Miss Thompson entered first, followed by my parents. I was right behind them. Mom turned around and said, 'Don't come in,' and then, 'Don't look.' But I was already inside and I saw Rex and then Opa."

She was shaking as she said, "It was hideous!"

"So sorry I had to make you go through this," I said.

"I already told it all to the policeman, but it's not any easier telling it again."

I nodded and then said, "I have to ask you one more thing. During the time you and your parents played Monopoly, did any of you leave the family room?"

She replied, "Mr. Knupp asked me that too. Mom had to go to the bathroom, and Dad said that since we were taking time out, he might as well call the bank and tell them that they could expect him back the next day. They were both gone for only a few minutes."

"Did you stay in the family room?"

"Yes, I did."

Then I asked, "When you first came downstairs with your father and walked along the corridor to the family room, was there anyone else around?"

"No, only Rex sitting in front of the train room," she answered.

"Was he calm at that time?"

"He wasn't barking, just wagged his tail when I petted him. He seemed a little spooked because of the storm, but then, so was I."

"Did anyone come into the room while the three of you played the board game?"

"I don't think so." Then she corrected, "Oh, Mrs. Schmied came in and said she'd already ran the vacuum, but would we mind if she quickly did the dusting. Then she moved around the place with her duster, but I didn't pay much attention since it was my turn to roll the dice. She didn't stay long."

Noticing that the girl was suppressing a yawn, I said, "We're done. I suspect you didn't get much sleep last night. Try to take a nap."

"I meant to sleep in the hammock before you showed up, but I was too upset." She got up and murmured, "Guess I'll go upstairs and try again."

Chapter 37

I watched her leave and then sat down on a patio chair and reflected on the information I'd gathered so far. The raging storm of the previous day was a thing of the past, the temperature had risen back to a level of pleasantly warm summer days, and the sky had turned blue again.

Erika came through the sliding glass door and plopped down next to me with a big sigh.

Motioning with her head toward inside, she said, "I need a break and some fresh air."

"Must be hard to make all the decisions," I remarked.

"That's for sure."

Then I asked, "Where is Rex? I'd like to take him for a walk."

"He's extremely upset. He was growling at Mr. Knupp this morning, so we put him in Papa's bedroom. You can't blame Rex for being resentful toward the police. As far as he's concerned, they're the ones that took his best friend away."

"Makes sense to a dog's mind."

"After Knupp left, I opened the door to Papa's room, but Rex wouldn't budge. I just checked again, and he's still sitting in the same spot on the rug next to the bed. He hasn't eaten since the tragedy either."

I said, "You've already given me a brief account of yesterday's events on the drive up, but I need more information from you."

"What do you want to know?"

"You told me the other day that at one time your father altered his will to benefit only you and Helga, and then apparently changed it back to its original state."

"That was years ago."

"I know, but try to be precise on this. When you told me about that will business, it wasn't clear to me. Did your father just threaten your brothers with making a new will to benefit you two women, or did he in fact make a new will and then later revert it back?"

She took some time to think this over and then finally said, "I don't remember. What difference does it make now? If he did make that will, he changed it back afterwards to benefit all of us again."

I didn't reply.

"Oh, I see! You think there might be the same pattern where this will in favor of Laura Thompson is concerned."

"Exactly."

"For heaven's sake, Regula! We'll soon find out from the estate lawyer, one way or another."

"Of course," I replied, "but it would help to get an idea of what the persons concerned think about the matter."

She just stared.

"The actual content of the current will is less important to me than what each person believes it contains."

"I see where you're headed now."

She seemed lost in thought for a long time and then exclaimed, "Something just occurred to me!"

"What's that?"

"Depending on what Laura Thompson thinks about the will, she might have a motive."

I remarked, "That was one of the first things that came to my mind, but unless she's an unusually good actress, she didn't take your dad's talk about a will in her favor seriously."

"Oh."

Then I asked, "Did your dad have a visitor yesterday, other than the family members?"

"Not that I know of. Why do you ask?"

"Mrs. Schmied claims she saw a stranger in the house yesterday morning."

"Claude dropped me off after we had my car towed to the mechanic, but he certainly didn't come inside. He just dropped me off and drove back down the hill. Ask Helga. She would know if anyone had been admitted into the house."

After a pause I said, "I hate to do this to you, but tell me the exact order of events after your father was discovered in the train room."

She nodded and then began, "I was working in my office when Mrs. Schmied burst in and said there had been an accident in the train room and she believed Papa was dead. It took a couple of seconds to register, and then I ran out the door, practically flew down the stairs, and rushed to the train room. When I got there, Alex, Mirella, Miss Thompson and Lotti were already in the room. I pushed past them and stopped in front of Papa and Rex. As I tried to get closer, Rex bared his teeth and growled. It was obvious he wouldn't let me near."

She took a deep breath before she continued, almost in a whisper, "From what I saw of Papa's face beneath the water, I was sure he was beyond help. Then I turned around, went out the door and called the authorities."

I looked into my friend's eyes and noticed they were moist. I silently took her into my arms, where she shook violently and sobbed.

Then she straightened up, saying, "I can't fall apart. I have too much to do." And she asked, "No more questions, right?"

"That was all."

"Then I'd better get back to the boys," she said, and left me.

I got up as well and went for a lonesome walk without the four-legged companion.

Chapter 38

An hour later when I wandered into the kitchen, Helga was bent over the stovetop stirring pasta sauce. I was shocked by her appearance as she glanced up. The housekeeper had aged years since I saw her last, only two days before. The lines around her mouth had deepened and her eyes expressed great suffering.

I grabbed a stool and sat down at the counter. "Can we talk while you fix dinner?"

Without enthusiasm she replied, "I'm just fixing spaghetti and sauce. I doubt anyone is really hungry."

I nodded. Then I said gravely, "I realize that yesterday's event hit you hard."

She didn't respond. I watched her filling a big pot with water, adding a handful of salt and a morsel of butter. She placed it on the electric burner and turned on the range.

She finally spoke, "I can't imagine Talblick without Otto Sonderegger."

"Hard to picture." Then I said, "Do you know why I came back?"

"To show your detective tricks," she answered, trying to sound funny but not succeeding.

"I need to know your movements of yesterday afternoon."

"I understand." I could tell it took a great effort to keep her tone matter of fact as she went on, "Let me see. I had lunch after the family finished eating. The cleaning woman, Rita Schmied, stopped by the kitchen and had a bite to eat as well. After clearing the dirty dishes away, I took inventory of the food in the fridge and pantry, deciding on menus for the next few days. It wasn't an easy task, since I didn't know how long the family guests were going to stay. I certainly wasn't going out to do the shopping in the rain, but I figured I might as well sit and write the list."

She continued, "Then later, I watered all the plants in the house and tended to the fresh flowers. By that time the storm was at its peak and thunder after thunder rattled the house. I was at the kitchen sink cutting off part of the rose stems from the dining room bouquet when I thought I heard Rex bark. I could've been mistaken, though, what with all the noise of the storm and Mrs. Schmied's vacuuming."

She paused, and then went on, "I was filling the vase of roses with fresh water when Rita   Schmied came in, blurting, 'Mr. Sonderegger drowned in his miniature lake. I'm sure he's dead!' I was so startled that I dropped the vase and it smashed on the floor, making a mess of broken glass, flowers and water. I didn't bother to clean up and ran to the train room. Halfway down the hallway Erika and Miss Thompson, followed by Alex and his family, were walking toward me. They all seemed in shock. I ran past them and kept going. The door to the train room stood open. I went in and - -"

She broke off, seemingly overwhelmed.

I said, "You don't need to go on. I know what scene you found there."

After a pause, I asked, "Did Mr. Sonderegger have any visitors yesterday other than his family?"

"Fritz Moritz dropped by."

"What time was that?"

"Around noon."

"Did you take him straight to your employer?"

"I just let him in the front door. Mr. Moritz knows his way around."

"How about earlier?"

"What do you mean?"

"Did anyone come to the mansion first thing in the morning?"

"No."

"Are you sure?"

She got annoyed with me, saying, "Aside from the family and staff, no one was admitted to the house yesterday morning. Why are you so persistent, Regula?"

"Rita Schmied said she saw a stranger in the hallway."

"A stranger? What did she mean by that?"

"Apparently, some man she'd never seen before."

"At what time did she say she saw that stranger?"

I answered, "After 9:00, but she had presumably heard him in conversation with Mr. Sonderegger before that time."

"Where?"

"In Sonderegger's office."

Helga stated, "Total nonsense! I admit, I came home late from a movie in Davos Sunday night, but I still got up before 7:00 yesterday. I certainly did not admit any stranger to the mansion. Unless the person had a key to the house, Schmied's statement just isn't true."

"Well, if you are this positive, the individual didn't come into the house via the front door. Maybe he let himself in through the veranda. I noticed that the sliding-glass door is unlocked during the day."

"Why should he? I'd presume anybody having business to discuss with Mr. Sonderegger would ring the front doorbell."

"Doesn't seem to make any sense."

She said, "If you ask me, Mrs. Schmied made it all up to make herself look important. She loves to gossip."

Then I asked, "Who of the staff was in the house?"

"Hans Weber, Laura Thompson, Rita Schmied, and me, of course."

"Who had a key to the mansion?"

"Only the three of us, Mr. Sonderegger, Erika and me. If any of the family guests plan to get home late, they borrow a key. Karl borrows mine often."

I nodded. "He's somewhat of a nocturnal creature, I've noticed."

Then I inquired, "I'm sure you're aware that Otto Sonderegger made a new will recently?"

"Yes, I heard."

"What is your opinion about it?"

She shrugged her shoulders and remarked, "I didn't pay much attention. He never kept it a secret that, no matter how many times he changed his will, I'd always be provided for."

"That's not what I meant. How do you feel about him disinheriting his sons?"

"It's none of my business, but I feel strongly that blood is thicker than water."

"I agree."

By that time Helga had added the spaghetti to the boiling water and was tossing a salad. She tasted the pasta for tenderness and then said, "Do you mind letting everyone know that dinner will be served in five minutes?"

"Not at all," I answered and applied myself to the task.

Chapter 39

After breakfast on Wednesday, I stepped out onto the veranda where Erika was talking on the phone. She had lists of names with phone numbers in front of her. I was passing by the patio table and chairs when she motioned for me to sit down next to her, which I did reluctantly. I felt awkward listening in as she told the person on the line, "We don't know yet. The police are investigating, of course." And after a pause, "The obituary will be in tomorrow's papers, but I felt that I should let you know in person. Thank you." She hung up and glanced at me. The last 42 hours had left their mark. She looked absolutely ghastly.

She said, "I wish people wouldn't ask so many questions. I know they mean well, but it's hard to take."

"Can I help you with anything?"

"Thanks for offering, but this is a family matter. We have to muddle through it ourselves."

"I understand."

Then she remarked, more to herself it seemed, "I wish I could just compose an e-mail and forward it to everyone. Sure would be a lot simpler, but I guess improper."

I asked, "Have you heard from Norbert?"

"No, and that might be a good sign."

"Really?"

"He should be busy with the auction as we speak. Since we haven't heard a word, I'd presume he's not under arrest."

Then I inquired, "Does Fritz Moritz live in Davos?"

"No, his house is right down the hill. Why?"

"I think I'll pay him a visit."

She said, "When you drive to Dörfli, just before you get to the main road there is a little unpaved side street to your right with only three houses. The second one is his. You're welcome to borrow my car again."

"Thanks, but it's a nice day. I'll walk."

Mirella and Alex stepped out onto the patio. Mirella addressed Erika, "We were just discussing going home for a couple of days and then coming back for the funeral, but we can't with a good conscience leave all the hassle to you. The funeral being on Saturday already, there are tons of arrangements to be made. As far as we know, Norbert is still in Basel, and you really cannot count on Karl being of any great help. So we're staying put."

Erika acknowledged the offer with a thankful glance and then asked her brother, "Can they manage at the bank without you?"

He answered modestly, "I'm not all that indispensable."

My friend said, "I appreciate your help. I've been contacting people since yesterday, and I've hardly made a dent in the list. Papa knew a lot of people. We also need to make more decisions as to where the memorial service is to be held as well as the meal afterward."

Mirella looked at me as if she hadn't noticed my presence before and said, "Hello! I don't know if 'Welcome back' is the appropriate thing to say under the circumstances."

I smiled and, getting to my feet, looked at her and Alex in turn, declaring, "If you get a chance, I'd like to interview you both. One at a time, please."

As I walked through the dining room and out to the hallway, Alex caught up with me and said, "Wait! I might as well get the questioning over with right away. Where do we go?"

"Your father's office," I replied.

Chapter 40

Suggesting Otto Sonderegger's office for having our talk was a spur of the moment decision. As we walked by the adjacent bedroom, I stood at the open door and glanced inside. Rex was sitting on the rug next to his late master's bed.

I took a few steps into the room and ordered, "Rex, come with us!" The dog raised his sad eyes at me. He didn't wag his tail, but he slowly got to his feet. I surveyed the poor animal and Mr. Sonderegger's words on the occasion of our first walk came to mind: "Rex would be lost without me!"

I repeated, "Come, Rex!" And the dog followed us into the office.

Surprised, Alex said, "You got him to move! As far as I know, he hasn't budged since yesterday morning."

When Knupp had summoned me to the office, I hadn't really taken notice of the room. At that time, I had walked straight to the desk, focusing my attention on the police officer in charge. Now I took a moment to look around. The place was gigantic, befitting the size of its late owner. To one side stood the sturdy oak desk with the brown leather chair behind. A single oak file cabinet sat in the corner. I noticed a door between the desk and the cabinet, presumably the connecting door leading to the bedroom. The other section of the room was furnished with a round table and four straight-back chairs grouped around it. Two area rugs covered the parquet floor, one at the desk area, and the other beneath the table and chairs. One wall was taken up with a floor-to-ceiling bookcase and the window stretched across the entire front of the office, from which one had a valley view. Decidedly a man's room, I mused, with no frills whatsoever.

We each grabbed a chair and sat at the round table. Rex flopped himself down between us on the area rug.

Alex took the initiative and said, "No offense, Regula, but I don't think Erika should have involved you in this. But since you're back and are obviously going to investigate, here is my two cents' worth. I'm sure you've noticed that we all quarreled a lot with Papa, but that was just on the surface. Deep down we loved him."

I didn't comment and waited for more to come.

He continued, "Norbert's unfortunate remark at lunch on the fatal day was a coincidence. My brother is incapable of violence."

I don't believe in coincidences as a rule, but I let it slide and asked him about his movements on Monday afternoon. His statements were in accord with those made by his daughter, except he was exact about the time they went down to the family room. He said he had just looked at his watch, and the time was 13:45, using the European time indication instead of a.m. and p.m.

I asked, "When you and your wife took time out from playing Monopoly, did you get back to the family room at the same time?"

"No, Mirella beat me to it."

"On your return, did you see or hear anyone?"

"I didn't see a soul. As for hearing, there wasn't much to be heard except the roaring of the storm."

"You didn't notice Rex?"

"Oh, of course. He was sitting in front of the train room. I thought you meant people."

"At what time did you hear screaming in the hallway and open the door to see what was going on?"

He replied, "I don't know, but it must have been shortly after 15:00. I checked the time later, when we followed Erika out of the train room after discovering Papa. It was 15:07 then."

I couldn't think of anything else to ask him and said, "That's a wrap. Thanks for talking to me."

The German shepherd's eyes followed him as he left, but the dog did not get up and stayed put next to me. As soon as the door closed behind Alex, I went across the room and found the connecting door unlocked. I opened it, and as expected, I had a view into the bedroom. I did not enter but surveyed the doorframe and door. It was thick and well constructed. I closed it again, rummaged in the desk drawer for notepaper and pen, and then went back to my chair and sat down. Rex had not moved from his spot on the area rug.

"Good boy, Rex!" I said.

Chapter 41

Minutes later, Mirella found me busily writing notes. I turned the notepad face down and was ready for the interview. She was dressed appropriately in black slacks and a white blouse. The expression on her face was somber, but the natural vitality in her gait was obviously more difficult to mask.

Before I had a chance to start the questioning, she said, "I still think my father-in-law met with a tragic accident. The idea that he was murdered is ridiculous."

I stated, "Accidental death is not a possibility. Mr. Knupp informed me that Otto Sonderegger had first been hit on the back of his head with a blunt instrument and then was drowned."

Her Italian temperament surfaced, and she threw up both her arms, saying, "Bah! What do the police know? They didn't see it happen. He could've hit his head someplace, knocking him unconscious, and then fallen into the water."

I didn't credit that with an answer, but asked her to give me an account of her whereabouts on Monday afternoon. Her story was a duplicate of what I had already learned from Lotti and Alex.

Then I queried, "When you interrupted the game to go to the bathroom, did you use the one in your room upstairs or one of the bathrooms on this floor?"

"I went upstairs," she replied.

"Did Alex also make his phone call from your bedroom?"

"Yes. He was still talking when I came down again."

Then I inquired, "Did you run across anyone on your way back to the family room?"

"No, I didn't."

"Did you hear anything apart from the sounds of the thunderstorm?"

"I think I heard the noise of a vacuum cleaner coming from somewhere."

"How much later than you did Alex get back to the family room?"

"Not much. Two or three minutes." Then she suddenly exploded, "This questioning is absurd!"

"Sorry, but I need to form a clear picture of events in order to investigate."

"The entire investigation is ludicrous! Take my word for it, no one in the Sonderegger family would have the nerve to commit murder."

"Would you?"

Dumbfounded, she asked, "Would I what?"

"You're not blood-related. Would you have the nerve to commit murder?"

She seemed to seriously think about this. Then she said, "Maybe under certain circumstances I'd kill. It would have to be a crime of passion, though. Certainly not for anything as common as money!"

"I'm far from having determined the motive in this case," I remarked.

Surprised, she said, "Oh? I thought the overall idea was that he was murdered because of the new will in favor of the Thompson woman."

Then I asked, "What did you think of your father-in-law?"

Without hesitation she replied, "One is not supposed to talk ill of the dead, but Otto Sonderegger was a thoroughly nasty old man. He took pleasure in tormenting his family. I'd have liked to tell him to go to hell."

"But you didn't?"

She shrugged. "Alex felt differently, and I stand by my man."

"An admirable trait," I commented.

She shrugged again.

After a pause, I suggested, "Would you help me with an experiment?"

"Certainly."

"Please go into your late father-in-law's bedroom through the connecting door. Close the door behind you and then just wait and listen. Don't come back until I tell you." She looked at me as if I were crazy but obeyed without comment.

I made sure she had closed the door securely and then went back to my seat. I asked in an average tone of voice, "How often do you hear from your son while he's in the *Rekrutenschule*? Does he like the military training?" Then I raised my voice just a tad and continued, "What did you purchase that day when you took Lotti shopping in Davos?" Finally, I brought up my voice to the approximate powerful volume of the late Sonderegger, saying, "How old are you, Mirella? Do you have any siblings?"

I crossed the room again and opening the connecting door, I said, "Come back, please, and answer all my questions."

She gave me a look of dismay and asked, "Are you playing games with me?"

"Not at all! I told you I was conducting an experiment. Please answer each question."

"There were only two. First I heard you mumble a few things but didn't catch the meaning. I'll answer the questions despite finding the first one rude. I'm forty-six. In reply to your other question, no, I'm an only child."

I said, "Thank you. You've helped a lot."

She eyed me keenly but didn't utter a word. I felt sure she thought of me as a feeble-minded old woman. She was still shaking her head as she walked out the door.

I bent down to Rex, and stroking his fur I remarked, "An interesting woman! What do you think?"

Chapter 42

In mid-afternoon on that Wednesday, I took off for Dörfli. Striding down the steep, curvy road, I couldn't help but being reminded of trekking that same way a few days earlier. Things had drastically changed since I had happily ambled toward the carnival on that previous day.

As directed, I turned right at the little dirt lane just above the village, then stood at the front door of the second house and rang the bell. Getting no response, I pushed the button again without result. Obviously, there was no one home.

I was just leaving when I heard Mr. Moritz's scratchy voice yelling from within, "Hold your horses, I'm coming!"

More time passed before the old man finally opened the door and appeared surprised to see me. He uttered, "Oh, Mrs. Huber, it's you! I thought you'd left the neighborhood by now." He motioned me to come in.

I followed as he hobbled slowly ahead. He led me to his living room and said, "I don't get around fast without my cane."

"Where do you keep it? I'll fetch it for you," I said.

"That's just it, I've misplaced it. I've been looking for the darned thing for two days!"

"Don't you have a spare?"

"I used to have a wooden one, but I can't find that one either. It's a pain to get old and forgetful."

Then he said, "How nice of you to look in on me! I don't have company often these days. Have a seat. I can't offer you any sodas, only cider or wine."

I hated to have him go to the trouble of limping to the kitchen and back, but I knew he would be offended if I refused his hospitality. Besides, I saw an open book, face down, sitting on the small side table by his chair, and I deemed some exercise might do him good.

So I said, "Cider sounds refreshing, thank you."

While he was out in the kitchen tending to the drinks, I looked around the room. Although old, the sofa group appeared well cared for. A bookcase was filled with hardcover editions and against the far wall stood a china hutch displaying decorative plates and knickknacks. A few pastel watercolors adorned the walls. The 27-inch TV set seemed the only modern piece of furniture in the room. There was an overall feminine touch to this living room, with doilies draped over chairs and furnishings. The place was clean but not tidy. I glanced at the title of the book my host had obviously been reading when I came to interrupt. It was *Arch de Triomphe* by Erich Maria Remarque, a novel not exactly the latest craze in fiction literature, but the old gentleman had good taste, I thought.

When he came back carrying a bottle of cider and two glasses, I complimented him, "I like your living room!"

"Thank you. I try to keep it picked up. My Anna always had the place spotless. I've left everything the way she had it arranged."

I took a sip from what I presumed was apple juice. It tasted sour, and I realized that it was alcoholic cider. I tried not to make a face.

Then I asked, "Apart from the domestic side, how are you getting along by yourself?"

"I'm lonely."

"I can well understand that."

He continued, "It was hard enough trying to deal with losing my Anna, and now my best friend is gone before we got a chance to reconcile."

"I'm glad you're bringing up Otto Sonderegger," I said, and explained the reason for my visit.

He heard me out, and then a sudden smile made his big mustache move, as the lip turned upward and his eyebrows rose. He chuckled, "You're an investigator? That's funny."

Then his expression became serious as he said, "The police were already here to question me yesterday."

"I hope you don't mind answering a few of mine?"

"No problem." And he added, "Knupp wanted to know all about the scene I caused when I burst in on the family at dinner confronting Otto. You were there, so you won't make me repeat it, I hope."

"Oh, no," I assured him, "I'm clear on that."

"Good."

"When did you see your friend for the last time?"

He looked pained when he replied, "On that evening when I interrupted your dinner."

"I was under the impression you saw him last on the day he was killed."

"Who told you that?"

"Helga said she admitted you to the mansion that day."

"Oh yes. I went up to Talblick on Monday, but I chickened out and never saw Otto."

"How did that come about?"

He scratched his bold head and said, "Otto called me several times and left messages on my answering machine after we had that fight last Friday night. I expected he wanted to apologize and make peace. So - -"

I interrupted, "You were never home when he called?"

"Of course I was home. Each time the phone rang I knew it must be him, so I didn't pick up. Who else would call me? Most of my friends and relatives have passed away. Anna and I didn't have any children."

He went on, "I wasn't ready to talk to him. I can be stubborn. The last message he left was Monday morning, telling me to bury the hatchet and come up to Talblick. He said something about unveiling the new section in the train room."

He sighed and continued, "I didn't know if I could forgive him, but I finally decided to go and have it out with him, once and for all. So I drove up and the housekeeper let me in. I was standing in the entrance-hall and heard the family talking in the kitchen, obviously having lunch. I was just about to go look for Otto when he apparently entered the kitchen from the dining room side. I heard him mocking and lecturing his family one by one. He seemed to be in a lousy mood, so I lost my nerve and decided this might not be a good day to tackle him. I left in a hurry, before he'd come out and spot me."

"I see." Then I asked, "At what time were you standing in the entrance-hall?"

"Around noon."

We didn't speak for a while, and I took a few more sips of cider. Then a totally different line of thought occurred to me, and I asked, "Did you park in the guest garage where the old stables used to be?"

"I usually do, but on Monday I left the car in the space near the front entrance. I didn't feel like walking all the way from the garage to the house on such a rainy day."

"I don't blame you."

Then I inquired, "How long had you known Otto Sonderegger?"

"A long time, nearly forty years."

"You became friends because you were neighbors?"

"No. We lived in Davos when he first hired me as chef at the Sondereggli. We moved to this house later."

"So you were his employee, but you also saw each other socially?"

"That's right. We got along great. The four of us had memorable times together," he replied.

"The four of you?"

"Sure, Otto and his Gypsy wife, my Anna and me." He chuckled as he added, "I never heard him call his wife by her name, which was Maria. He always referred to her as Esmeralda or his fiery Gypsy. Maria used to sing and dance during high season at the Sondereggli. She was an excellent performer."

I thought he had forgotten why I was there as he reminisced further, "Otto and Maria were well matched. She was one of the few people he couldn't control, and I think he admired her for that. They seemed to have a perfect marriage, but Maria was definitely a free spirit. Still, it came as a big surprise to everybody when she just up and left one day. Otto would never admit it, but I knew he was totally crushed and hurt for many years. Anna missed her too. Regardless of their age difference, the two women had hit it off."

It was a warm afternoon, and I was thirsty. After the first few nips the cider hadn't tasted all that bad, so I kept drinking. By the time Mr. Moritz came to a stop with reliving his past, he refilled my glass.

Then he came back to the present and said, "I wish I'd stayed and faced him on Monday. We might have made peace. Now I have to live with myself remembering only my last angry words spoken to my friend." He paused and then said, "Most of all, I wish I'd never found Anna's diary. My life has become even more miserable since I stumbled on the damned journal than it already was before."

I felt bad for the old gentleman and changed the subject. "Are you also eighty-four?"

"No. I'm two years younger than Otto was."

"How long have you been retired?"

"Twelve years. I retired the year I turned seventy."

"Was that when Mr. Sonderegger sold his hotels?"

He smiled and said, "Otto held out a lot longer. At that time he was still hoping his grandson would take over the business one day. Otto only sold out five years ago."

"I see."

Then I said, "I think we covered all I needed to know. Thank you for talking so freely with me and thanks for the cider." Pointing to the little table next to his chair, I remarked, "I'll let you get back to *Arch de Triomphe* now."

When I got to my feet, I felt a little dizzy. That cider must have been more potent than I realized.

Mr. Moritz started to get up too, and I quickly said, "Please don't bother to see me to the door."

Smiling, he answered, "Are you sure? It seems to me the lady investigator might be slightly tipsy!"

Chapter 43

By the time I had hiked halfway up the hill, the effect of the cider had switched from my head to my bladder. I wished I had asked to use Mr. Moritz's bathroom before leaving his house. I seriously contemplated going behind a bush when I heard a car approaching. I turned around, and sure enough, there was Karl's red Porsche coming around the curve below. It abruptly came to a halt by my side, and the young man rolled down his window and yelled above the sound of the running motor, "On the road again, Mrs. Huber! Want a lift?"

I nodded and walked around the car to the passenger side. Getting in, I said, "You're a Godsend!"

He smirked and declared, "I've heard that said to me just a few nights ago!"

Then he stepped on the gas, and we sped up to Talblick. His lighthearted, joking manner didn't fool me. I had seen the apprehensive look in his eyes when I'd entered the car.

Then he asked, "Did you have a purpose in going down to Dörfli, or do you just enjoy hiking?"

"I paid Mr. Moritz a visit," I answered.

He whistled and said, "Aha, I caught the sleuth at work! How is your investigation coming along?"

"I have some ideas, but they're still vague at this point."

"I'll bet you've got lots of ideas. You're a sharp lady."

When he let me out in front of the house, I said, "Speaking of my investigation, I'd like to interview you if you have the time."

"I always have plenty of time. Let me just put my little red horse in the stable, and then I'll be all yours. Where's headquarters?"

"In your dad's office," I informed him.

Chapter 44

Karl was waiting for me, reclined in a chair with his arms folded behind the neck and his feet up on the round table. When he saw me come in, he slid the feet off the furniture and sat up straight. I grabbed the chair next to him.

I said, "Now then, tell me about your movements on Monday from noon until your father's body was discovered."

He smiled and remarked, "I see you're wasting no time and getting straight to the point!" Then he said seriously, "There isn't much to tell. I came down from my room a few minutes after 12:00 to have something to eat. When I got to the kitchen, the others were already having lunch, so I joined them."

"Who are 'the others'? Please be precise."

"Okay. My sister, brothers, Mirella and the kid."

"Your dad wasn't there?"

"No."

"Please continue."

"As I said, I joined them for lunch. Afterward, we all went our separate ways. I headed back to my room, listened to music and promptly dozed off. I needed to catch up on my sleep. I came home late the night before. Besides, there wasn't much else to do on a rainy day."

He paused and then continued, "Next thing I knew, Sis knocked at my door, shouting, 'Karl! Are you there?' and before I was fully conscious, she burst in on me and told me the bad news."

I waited. When the silence started to get uncomfortable, I said, "Please go on."

"That's it. I have nothing more to contribute. Obviously, nobody witnessed my nap. You'll just have to take my word for it."

"Didn't you come to the train room to see for yourself what happened after Erika told you the news?"

"Of course! I hurried down, but the police wouldn't let me into the room to see Papa. When I got there, two men carried Rex out. I thought the dog was dead. Later, when we all had to assemble in the living room waiting to be interrogated by Knupp, I found out that he had only been drugged. I tried again to go in to see Papa, but as I said, the authorities were in the room. One policeman stood guard at the door and barred my way."

I remarked, "In a way you were fortunate to have been spared the shocking sight."

He reflected, and then said, "I guess that's true, but it makes his death unreal to me. What I mean is, I still don't want to believe it."

He became grave as he said, "I'm an irresponsible guy, and I might never become responsible and settle down. Regardless, unlike my brothers, I didn't respond to Papa's customary summons out of fear of what he might do to me if I wouldn't abide by his wishes. I always came because I knew Papa was basically a lonesome man. Sure, he had Erika, and Rex never left his side, but I know he craved the companionship of all his sons. He never would've admitted this, of course."

I was surprised by this young man's insight. On the surface he gave the impression of being a carefree and flippant playboy, but apparently there was more to him than met the eye.

After a short pause he went on, "Papa was pissed off that none of us were interested in taking over the hotel business. For years he fought back by making a game out of taunting each one of us with our respective weaknesses. Alex mostly ignored him, and when Papa's comments did bother him, he tried not to show it. Norbert was an easy target. I'm sure you've noticed that yourself."

"I certainly have." Then I smiled and said, "And you handled his needling by humoring him. Am I right?"

He seemed to revert back to his breezy nature and said mischievously, "You bet. And in my case, everything Papa complained about was true!" Then he sighed and said, "I'm going to miss the old tyrant."

I asked, "When did you see your father last?"

"On Sunday evening, before I drove to Davos for a night out."

"You didn't see him on Monday, the day he was killed?"

He shook his head.

"What time did you get home from your Sunday nightlife?"

"I didn't look at my watch, but it was the next morning."

"Was it already daylight?" I asked.

"Definitely."

"Did you encounter anyone on the road from Dörfli to Talblick on the way up?"

"No. Should I have?"

"Oh, just a thought."

Then I inquired, "How is Natasha doing?"

"Who?"

"Your friend from Friday night," I replied.

"Oh, her. I'm sure she's doing fine."

After he left, I worked on making notes. I had learned a lot from my interviews so far, but deciding which were important facts and which were irrelevant would not be an easy task. For the time being, I jotted down all the data

I had gathered, no matter how insignificant some of it seemed.

Chapter 45

In the evening, Peter called, and before I could get a word in edgewise, he demanded, "Where the heck are you? Are you okay? I get to Zurich thinking you're waiting for me. Instead, your sister tells me she hasn't seen nor heard from you. She only received a strange call from Erika requesting your number and then hung up without explaining. What's going on, Regula?"

I said, "In answer to your first question, I'm at Talblick, and - -"

"You mean you haven't even been to Bad Ragaz?"

"I was there, but yesterday Erika begged me to come back. Let me explain," and I told him the sordid news.

He said, "How appalling! I'm sorry about the old man, but surely Erika has enough family standing by and doesn't need your moral support!"

"You don't understand. She hired me to look into the murder."

"What? I don't believe this! We're on vacation, for crying out loud!"

"I'm sorry, Peter."

He raged on, "This is ridiculous. Have you lost all sense of proportion? I'm sure the Swiss police are more than capable. Let them handle it. I suggest you take the next train to Zurich."

"I couldn't just say 'no' to Erika. She thinks the authorities suspect one of her brothers. She is desperate."

I heard him take in his breath. Then he said, "What about our plans to travel on to Eastern Europe? I'm sure you're aware that we don't have unlimited time on our hands before we must fly home!"

"I'm really sorry, Peter. You'll have to continue the trip without me."

"You're the one who wanted to see Prague so badly!"

"I know, and I hate to miss out on it, but I need to stay here. Try to understand."

He sighed, saying, "Well, I'm certainly not traveling to Eastern Europe without you. We'll just have to postpone it indefinitely."

"I feel guilty to have ruined our plans, but I'm committed to investigate this case."

"Obviously!" Then he seemed to get his composure back and said, "How long do you think this investigation of yours will take?"

"I don't know."

"I hope you haven't forgotten that we're flying home a week from tomorrow. I expect you to be on that plane."

"Me too."

Then he asked, "Do you want me to come?"

"Oh no. That's not necessary."

"Good. I'd rather spend the rest of my vacation without getting involved with your crime household."

I inquired, "Where are you planning to go now?"

"You haven't given me any time to make new plans," he replied. And I knew his natural good humor was fully restored when he added, "For starters, I'm going to hang around Zurich for a couple of days and check out all your favorite spots in Old Town!"

Laughing, I remarked, "Thanks for rubbing it in!" Then I said, "Would you do me a favor?"

"First you spoil our trip and now you ask for favors?" he teased.

"I only packed a small suitcase before I came here and left the big one in Zurich. I'm running out of clothes to wear. I'd appreciate if you'd take a few items out of the big bag and send them to me."

"You're kidding!"

"I'm serious, Peter. I'll tell you what to look for, and you can send it via train. The package should reach me in one day."

"Regula! Don't be absurd. I'm sure they're letting you use the washer and dryer, or you can rinse your underwear out in the sink."

"It's not a matter of underwear. I don't want to wear the same outfits over and over again."

He exclaimed, "Go buy yourself new outfits, then! I'm not about to rummage through the suitcase for *items*."

I said, "Why, thank you, dear! No limit?"

"You're the biggest con artist this side of the ocean!"

On that note we ended the call.

Chapter 46

Talking with a few people in Davos was on my agenda for the next day. I had declined Erika's offer to drive me there, but I did ask her to call Hans Weber and Laura Thompson to explain the reason for my visits. As for Claude Boreau, I had looked him up in the phone book and planned to drop by unannounced. I did not mention my intention to interview him to Erika. I knew she would object, so I spared myself the hassle.

On the short train ride from Dörfli to Davos, I overheard a couple of ladies chatting who sat directly behind me. The first one said, "Amazing how hot the weather turned all of a sudden."

The other replied, "We're lucky to live up here, though. The heat is apparently unbearable at a lower altitude. In Zurich they're experiencing temperatures of 28 to 33 degrees!"

I couldn't help but smiling. 28 to 33 degrees Celsius would be from the low 80s to about 92 Fahrenheit. These women had no idea what "heat" was!

Upon leaving the train station at Davos Platz, I followed Erika's directions to Weber's place of business. Getting lost in Davos was virtually impossible, as the twin towns of Davos Platz and Davos Dorf comprised two long main streets, both one-way. One was Talstrasse, leading from Platz to Dorf and the other, Promenade, going from Dorf to Platz.

I ambled along Talstrasse and, passing the Church of St. John the Baptist, remembered having once stepped inside the old house of worship when in my teens. The nave dated back to 1285. I recalled having been particularly impressed with a window in the choir created by Augusto Giacometti. Then I strolled by the town hall, another old structure, and a couple of blocks further turned into a cross street.

The building I was looking for housed several small businesses. According to the directory, the tenants on the ground floor consisted of a graphics design firm, a hair salon and a florist. Weber shared the second floor with an interior decorating outfit and a dentist. I took the elevator to the second story. The sign at his door read, "Hans Weber, Physical Therapy and Massage."

I entered the small waiting room. There was no receptionist, but as soon as I closed the door behind me, a recording of the masseur's voice announced, "Please be seated. I'll be with you shortly." I sat down and selected a sports magazine from a stack of journals arranged on the coffee table. I was a few minutes early for my appointment, but I didn't have to wait long. Soon, a middle-aged man opened the inner door and walked through the waiting room. He appeared totally drained.

As he passed me on his way out, I smiled and said, "You'll feel great in an hour or two!"

"I know," he replied. Evidently, this had not been the first time Hans Weber had pounded his body.

Then the blond giant himself stuck his head in, saying, "Come in, Mrs. Huber."

I advanced to the interior. The place was large, sporting diverse gym-equipment on one side and a massage table on the other. At the far end of the room stood a small sofa group.

He led me to that corner and mentioned, "I don't have an office."

We sat down, and I asked, "You're a one-man outfit?"

"Yes."

"We have something in common, then. My business in the States is also a one-person deal."

"Uh-huh."

I continued, "I'm sure Erika Graff told you what my business is about and the reason I'm here to see you today?"

"Uh-huh."

Oh no! I thought. I'll get "uh-huh" answers throughout the entire interview.

Aloud I said, "I hope you can help me with my investigation."

He answered, "The police already questioned me."

"Yes, of course, but please go over it with me once more."

"All right."

"Tell me about your day at the mansion on Monday."

"I drove up, gave Otto Sonderegger his massage, washed the sheets and towels and drove back to Davos."

Had I really expected a more detailed account of his movements? He left me no choice but to drag information out of him, piece by piece.

So I asked, "At what time did you get to Talblick?"

"At 9:30."

"Where did you park your car?"

"In the guest garage."

"Did you see anyone on your drive up to Talblick either in a car or on foot?"

"No, but a car was parked on the last turnout."

"Really?"

He didn't elaborate, so I probed, "Was that unusual?"

He shrugged and said, "It didn't block the road, so it was none of my concern."

There was not a curious bone in this young man's body, I decided.

"Did you recognize the car?"

"No."

"Who did you see when you got to the mansion?"

"Helga Hodler let me in. The kid talked to me, and of course I saw Mr. Sonderegger."

"You talked to Lotti?"

"Uh-huh."

"Please tell me where and at what time you talked to her. I would also appreciate hearing what you chatted about."

"I was waiting for Mr. Sonderegger in the massage room. I had left the door open and the kid walked in. She was obviously bored. She asked me what was involved in a full body massage. So I told her."

I inquired, "At what time did you give Mr. Sonderegger the massage?"

"At 10:30," he replied.

"Was that his usual time for having it?"

"Most days he had it around 9:30, but there were exceptions."

"What was the reason for the exception on Monday?"

"He took Rex for a walk first, while it had stopped raining."

I nodded and then asked, "Was Mr. Sonderegger pleasant to work for?"

"What do you mean?"

"Was he easy to get along with?"

He stated, "We didn't engage in small talk. I gave him physical therapy and massages for which he paid me well."

I remarked, "It must have been hard for you to schedule your appointments around Otto Sonderegger, since you couldn't always be sure how much time you'd spend at Talblick."

"Not at all. Mr. Sonderegger hired me two years ago for physical therapy and later to give him daily massages. I knew my job with him would be on a long-range basis, so he took top priority. Most days I had early morning appointments here, so I seldom got to Talblick before 9:30. I was usually done at the mansion by 12:00 or 13:00, so my afternoons were open for other commitments."

Bravo! The man was capable of uttering more than one-syllable words.

Aloud I asked, "What kind of mood did Mr. Sonderegger seem to be in when you gave him Monday's massage?"

"I wouldn't know."

"That's right, you didn't engage in small talk!"

My sarcastic remark was totally lost on him. So I inquired further, "What did you do after you were through with the massage?"

"I went to the laundry room to wash and dry the dirty linens I'd used."

"Did you always take care of those sheets and towels yourself?"

"Yes."

"At what time did you leave the house?"

"At 14:15. I was running later than usual, but it didn't matter. I had no other appointment until 16:00 that afternoon."

Then I inquired, "Did you see anyone while tending to the laundry?"

"Lots of people."

I waited for him to go on. When it became clear that he was not going to comment further, I said, "Whom did you see?"

"Schmied moving around with her vacuum cleaner. Mr. Moritz was standing in the entrance-hall at noon. Later, Hodler was in the kitchen when I passed by, and

when I carried my last load back to the massage room, I
got a glimpse of the Italian lady walking down the hall. I
think she went into the family room."

"Mirella Sonderegger?"

"Uh-huh."

I continued, "Did you see Mr. Sonderegger after you
were through with his massage?"

"No, but later in the afternoon Rex was sitting in front
of the train room, so he must've been in there."

"Who informed you of the tragedy?"

"The police, when they came to question me."

"Must've been a great shock to you."

"Uh-huh."

"Have you formed an opinion of who the killer might
be?"

"No." And he looked me in the eye and said, "Certainly
not me. I've lost a most valuable client."

Then I asked, "Did you know about Mr. Sonderegger's
will?"

"His will is none of my business," he replied.

"What I meant is, did you hear about the rumor that he
left his money to Laura Thompson?"

"I don't listen to rumors."

I thanked him for his time, and getting to my feet, I
took the piece of paper with Claude Boreau's address out
of my purse. "Do you know where this is?"

"Uh-huh. It's not far from here," and he gave me
directions.

Chapter 47

The receptionist at the chiropractor's place of business was in her early twenties and cute. She was browsing through a fashion magazine and ignored me at first, so I took a seat.

She suddenly looked up and asked, "Can I help you?"

I replied, "I'd like to see Claude Boreau, please."

"Do you have an appointment?"

"No, I don't."

"He's with a patient."

"I'll wait."

She gave me a scrutinizing look. Then she informed me, "If you're new, you must fill out a patient form. He might be able to squeeze you in later in the day."

As she searched in her desk for the appropriate form, I said, "I'm not a patient, but he knows me. When he has a minute, just tell him R.A. Huber would like to talk to him."

She nodded and then buried her head in the journal again. Twenty minutes later, a man, presumably the patient, walked by and left. Then the receptionist disappeared.

When she came back, she said, "This way please," and I followed her through a door and down a small hallway. Her skirt was extremely short, showing off her shapely legs.

She led me to a room, motioned me in, saying, "Have a seat. Mr. Boreau will be right with you," and retreated.

I sat down in the chair facing the large mahogany desk and thought, unlike Hans Weber, the chiropractor not only boasted a receptionist but an office as well.

Boreau seemed surprised to see me. *"Madame Uber!* I thought you had left us," he said in French.

"I had, but Erika implored me to come back." I replied, also in French. We were obviously not going to converse in anything else.

"Why would she do that?"

"You've heard about her father's murder?"

"Yes, Erika told me. She pretends to be brave, but I know that she is devastated."

"Did she tell you that she hired me?"

He seemed puzzled. "Hired you?" And after a pause, "Oh, I see! You are doing the sleuthing. No, she didn't mention it."

Then his green eyes fixed me with an appraising stare as he said, "So you're working on this homicide. Are the police not doing a good job, then?"

"I'm sure they're conducting an excellent investigation, but extra manpower, so to speak, is always an asset."

"Or, in your case, womanpower," he retorted.

I said, "Speaking of the police, did they question you?"

"No. Why should they?"

"But you don't mind if I do?"

"Go ahead, but I doubt that I can help you. I know nothing of the Talblick household. Erika keeps her home life private."

"I understand she spent Sunday night at your apartment."

He grinned and remarked, "I can see she keeps no secrets from you!"

"She also told me that you dropped her off at the mansion Monday morning."

"That is correct."

"At what time was that?"

"I don't remember exactly. Before 9:30, I think."

"Did you park the car and walked her to the door?"

"No, I just let her out at the front entrance."

"You didn't go into the house or anywhere else on the estate?"

He hesitated and then said, "I did not go into the house."

"But?"

He took a moment before he responded, "Oh, what the heck, I might as well tell you. Don't blab this to Erika, she'd get mad. It had stopped raining, so I decided to have a look around. I was curious to check out the tennis court. I didn't want to leave the car parked in front of the mansion because Erika was liable to look out a window. A little ways down the hill there is a turnout in the road, so I drove down to it and parked the car there. Then I hiked the short distance back to the mansion. I found the tennis court behind the house. It's a great court and well kept, by the way. What a shame people rarely play on it anymore!"

"I agree with you there," I commented.

Then I asked, "How long did you stay on the grounds?"

"Not long. Maybe ten minutes, fifteen at most. While looking over the court, I heard a car and then saw it being driven to some structure beyond the court. I didn't necessarily want to be seen, so I felt I'd better get going and turned back."

"On the road to and from Talblick, did you encounter anyone?"

"No one drove from the opposite direction either time, but I saw a hiker on my way down."

"Tell me more about the hiker."

"I was close to Dörfli, having just driven around the last curve before the first houses appeared, when he came out of the shortcut and onto the road. I was thinking that he must've been a dedicated hiker, tramping around on the muddy ground with the rain apt to start at any moment again."

"Did you get a good look at him?"

"Not really. I first saw him from the side, and then only from the back as he walked along the road before I passed him."

I inquired, "It was a man?"

"Yes, definitely," he replied.

"But you can't describe him?"

"He was tall, but that's all I can tell you. I didn't see his face and, frankly, I didn't pay much attention to him."

"And he was hiking down, in the direction of Dörfli?"

"Yes. He must have taken the shortcut which ended where I saw him come out."

I nodded. Then I got up and said, "Thank you for taking the time to talk to me, Monsieur Boreau."

"Enchanté, Madame Uber!"

Chapter 48

My lunch date with Laura Thompson was scheduled for an hour later near where she lived in Davos Dorf. Not pressed for time, I opted for a hike instead of taking the bus to the restaurant. To avoid the hustle and bustle of going through the center of town, I chose to take a stroll via the Hohe Promenade, also known as *Eichhörnliweg*, which translates as Squirrel Way.

I started off by climbing the steep path that led to the Catholic *Marienkirche*. Arriving at the top of the hill, I paused to catch my breath, and then the walkway leveled out, giving me a leisurely saunter for the rest of the way. The trail guided me underneath trees where curious squirrels came rushing down the trunks, begging for food. I had nothing to offer but watched as a couple with two little kids fed them. The small animals were not a bit shy and quickly grabbed the treats presented from the children's outstretched palms.

Half a mile into my walk I ambled along a wooden bridge, serving as overpass for the cable railway leading up to the *Schatzalp*, and then stopped at the edge of the bridge to admire the fabulous view. Straight across the valley I gazed at the *Jakobshorn* ski area and to the left the *Pischa*. Then I looked downward and surveyed the entire town of Davos. The imposing ice stadium stood out and immediately caught my eye. This is where, between Christmas and New Year, the world-famous *Spenglercup* takes place. Hockey teams from all over Europe, the United States and Canada compete during the event. Next to the stadium was the *Kongresshaus*, where Erika and I had enjoyed listening to Bach and Mozart music and where, every January, the global VIP's gather for the World Economic Forum. I also spotted the giant waterslide of the water-adventure park that Erika told me about called *Eau là là*.

I strolled on past the children's clinic for treatment of skin allergies and childhood obesity, and soon arrived at the small waterfall that flows into the *Schiabach* stream. The creek divides Davos Platz and Davos Dorf. Next I ambled by the former lung-sanatorium *Albula*, which is now a youth hostel since the tuberculoses battle has been virtually won.

I came upon the *Parsenn* funicular, which climbs to the famous *Parsenn* ski area. Oh, how I wished it were winter!

The *Hohe Promenade* ended when I reached the church of St. Theodul in Davos Dorf. I checked my watch and decided it was time to meet the court reporter.

Chapter 49

A somber Laura waited for me inside the Italian restaurant. She was already seated at a little table for two and waved me over as I paused near the entrance. She clearly looked distressed.

I took the seat facing her, and after exchanging greetings we studied the menu.

She said, "Pizza sounds good. I haven't had any since I left the States."

"It has been a while for me too. That's settled then. We order pizza." And winking at her I mentioned, "We'll have to eat it with knife and fork, you know."

"You're kidding?"

"Finger food is virtually unacceptable in Europe."

A gentleman got up from the table next to ours, walked over and stopped next to Laura, commenting in perfect English, "Your friend is wrong. The pizza will be served to you in one piece, but you're allowed to cut it into slices yourself and eat it by hand, if you wish." That said, he went back to his seat.

I shrugged my shoulders. "Okay, then," I said, laughingly.

The waiter appeared and we gave our order.

Then I said, "Have you formed any plans yet?"

"Plans?" she asked uncomprehendingly.

"Under the circumstances, you might be thinking of going home?"

"Oh, I see." After a pause she replied, "I was looking forward to the next ski season, but yes, I think now I'm going home as soon as possible."

"That might be for the best." Then I said, "I know Erika forewarned you about this interview, but what exactly did she tell you about me?"

"Not much. Mrs. Graff said that you are a private investigator and she hired you to look into the matter." And with an attempt at humor she remarked, "I've lost my job, and it seems you've inadvertently gained one!"

"Yes, not necessarily my idea of a European vacation."

"But you feel you owe it to your friend?" she asked.

"Precisely."

At that point the waiter brought the pizza, and we concentrated on eating it without regard to fork and knife.

Then I said, "I need to question you about Monday."

"Yes, of course."

"Tell me your movements from the time you arrived at Talblick until Mr. Sonderegger's body was discovered. Try to remember the exact time and order of each happening."

She said, "He called about 9:30 in the morning and asked me to come to the mansion at noon. So I left Davos at 11:30 and got there a few minutes before 12:00. Ms Hodler admitted me to the house, and I walked straight to the room where I usually worked."

I put in, "I call it the dictating room."

She smiled and continued, "So I walked straight to the dictating room, set up my steno machine, inserted a new roll of paper and waited for the boss. He soon came and seated himself in his chair with Rex settling at his feet. First he had me read back two entire previous chapters. Then he told me that he wanted to dictate something from the present, although we were still decades in the past with the memoirs. He explained he wanted me to take it down now, while it was still fresh in his mind. Later, when we'd finally get to the present, I could insert whatever he was about to dictate.

"I told him, 'No problem,' and he started dictation. He only got to the first sentence, however, altering it at least three times. Then he seemed to get frustrated and said, 'I've changed my mind. I can't concentrate right now. I'll get back to you after I'm done in the train room. So stick around.' I told him again, 'No problem.' Then he jumped up and left with Rex close on his heels."

I asked, "Did you get the impression that your employer was in a bad mood?"

She reflected and then answered, "He wasn't in one of his better dispositions. The weather might have had something to do with it."

"Were his moods influenced by weather?"

"Maybe it was just coincidence, but he appeared to be in a joking state of mind more often on a sunny day and cranky when it rained." With a remembering little smirk she added, "And during the span of a full moon, he seemed at his most witty, sarcastic self!"

Then I inquired, "What was that first sentence he dictated? Do you remember?"

She answered, "He changed it so many times, I'm not sure what we ended up with. It surely didn't reveal anything of the subject matter he had in mind."

"I'd like to know anyhow. Please try to recall his words."

"Okay. He started with Monday's date and told me to use the date instead of a chapter number. The idea was to eventually replace the date with the appropriate chapter once we got to the current time of the memoirs. Anyhow, all I have is Monday's date and the first sentence, which goes something like this: 'Today, out of the clear blue, I was faced with deceit.' As I said, that sentence doesn't tell us a thing."

"No, it certainly doesn't." And I asked, "The two chapters he had you read back to him, were they where you had left off the previous Friday?"

She had to think it over, and then said, "One of them was from Friday, and the other went back to Thursday. It was not where we had left off, though. He had dictated a total of three chapters on Friday." And she explained, "That was not an uncommon request, by the way. Mr. Sonderegger had me read back earlier chapters frequently. That's one of the reasons why the writing of his memoirs moved along at such a slow pace."

"Well, it appears you had a productive day on that Friday. Three chapters in a day seems a lot," I remarked.

"He went through one of his prolific spurts."

"I see." Then I said, "Sorry I sidetracked you. Please continue with Monday's events."

"Where was I? Oh yes, Mr. Sonderegger left. Then - -"

I interrupted again, "Sorry, but at what time did he leave the dictating room?"

"I didn't check the time. Let me see. He came in a few minutes past noon. Then he had me search for the two appropriate chapters, which took maybe five minutes. Reading them back to him might have taken half an hour, as one of them was long. His explanations about a current event he wanted to dictate, followed by his phrasing and rephrasing that one sentence, took another ten minutes. I would say he left shortly before 1:00 p.m."

She went on, "Once on my own, I had some more editing to do from the Friday before. As I told you, Mr. Sonderegger dictated for hours on that day. It was time-consuming work. I frequently had to consult the dictionary, since my German spelling isn't always up to par. I finished editing and printing out the last pages at 2:55 p.m."

She smiled and said; "I do know the time precisely, since I looked at my watch when I was finally done."

"You said you printed out pages. Do you have an actual paper copy of the memoirs, then?"

"Definitely," she replied, "Mr. Sonderegger insisted that I keep a current paper copy of the manuscript. He liked to browse through it, occasionally pointing out spelling errors."

"I see."

She continued, "Then I decided to back everything up onto the disc before I'd forget, since I'd brought the disc along."

I asked, "You don't keep your back-up disc in the dictating room?"

"No. It's at my aunt's house." And she sheepishly admitted, "I didn't back up nearly as often as I should have. Sometimes I forgot to bring the disc along."

"Why not just keep it at Talblick?"

She shrugged and said, "I guess that routine goes back to my training. At the court reporting school we were told that for safety reasons we should always keep the back-up disc in a different location from the transcript. I don't think it would've mattered much here, one way or the other, but old habits are hard to break."

She kept going, "While copying the manuscript to the disc, I heard Rex bark. I figured he was uneasy because of the storm raging. The thunder and lightning was ferocious by that time. A minute or two later, I heard screaming in the hallway and came out to check what was going on. I almost collided with Mrs. Schmied. She was shrieking at the top of her lungs running past me, while pointing down the hall toward the train room. I hurried along the corridor.

Alex Sonderegger and his family were coming from the opposite direction. We got to the train room about the same time. I stepped inside first, with Alex Sonderegger and his wife and daughter right behind me."

She shuddered, and then said, "I'll never forget the horrible scene we faced in there." And after a pause she remarked sadly, "Even though Rex was guarding him, I could tell we were too late. Mr. Sonderegger seemed clearly dead."

I nodded.

"I think we were all in shock. Mrs. Graff came into the room shortly afterward. The rest of us automatically stepped back to let her through. It was obvious that Rex wouldn't even allow Mrs. Graff any closer to the old man than a couple of feet. She stood by her dad and the dog for some time, keeping very still. Then she suddenly turned around and walked away. I followed her out, and I think the Alex Sonderegger family did likewise. In the hallway we passed Ms Hodler, who was apparently on her way to the train room."

She sighed and continued, "That's about it. Soon the police arrived and we had to assemble in the living room, from where we were called into Mr. Sonderegger's office for questioning, one by one."

Our plates were taken away, and we ordered coffee. We refrained from speaking for some time, each lost in our own worlds, it seemed.

Laura broke the silence and remarked, "It's most upsetting. Mr. Sonderegger was in excellent health for his age. He would've lived for many more years."

"True."

She shared her feelings further, saying, "I really liked the old man. I respected him for all his many accomplishments in life, but that wasn't really what mattered most. When you got beyond his gruff and controlling shell, you found a compelling human being at the core. He could also be witty and entertaining, if he chose." And with a little smile she added, "He called me *Magic Fingers*."

"Yes, I know."

I paid for the meal, and as we got up to leave, Laura commented, "I hope to God you'll catch the lousy killer."

"I'll do my best," I replied.

We parted in front of the place. I boarded a bus to take me back to Davos Platz and then applied myself to some serious shopping.

Chapter 50

Hours later, Erika picked me up at the Dörfli train station.

On the drive up the hill she stated, "I have two things to tell you. Number one, the police are back and they're turning Talblick up side down. Second, I'm mad at you!"

"Tell me about number two first," I said.

"You had no business to question Claude. That was totally unnecessary."

"So he already told you about it. That was fast," I retorted.

"Don't evade the subject, Regula. Why did you go see him behind my back?"

"What would have been your reaction if I'd told you in advance?"

"I'd have forbidden it," she replied.

"There's your answer!"

After a pause, I said, "So the police are back?"

"They came right after you left this morning. They conducted another house search and are hunting the grounds again. They're still at it now. I have no idea what they're looking for. I thought they were done with the search on Tuesday. I had to lock Rex up again, poor thing. Not that he takes much interest in his surroundings any longer. He's still not eating."

"I have compassion for that dog," I remarked.

Then she asked, "How are you coming along with the investigation?"

"I've talked to everyone except Norbert. People have given me tons of information, but I still can't see my way clearly. I'll get there, Erika. Please bear with me."

"What else can I do?" she said, discouraged.

Two vehicles were parked in front of the mansion. One was a marked police car and the other belonged to Knupp.

Pointing to the latter, Erika said, "That reminds me. He wants to talk to you."

Chapter 51

I sat opposite Herr Knupp at the late Sonderegger's desk once more. He still boasted a few unruly strands of hair sticking up on top of his head. Must be his trademark, I gathered.

He said, "Before I forget, you can have this back," and he handed me my passport.

Grabbing it, I remarked, "So you've checked me out?"

"You've passed muster." Then he inquired, "Have you made any progress with your *private* investigation?"

"I've learned a lot from the people I've talked to, but as far as coming to any conclusions, I'm still fumbling in the dark."

"Let me know when you see a glimmer of light."

I asked, "You haven't made an arrest yet. Correct?"

"What makes you think that?"

"You misunderstand. I don't think any such thing, but my friend was worried that her brother may have been arrested in Basel."

"We did question Norbert Sonderegger a second time in Basel to get certain facts straight." And after a pause he added, "We have no evidence to arrest anyone at this point in time."

"I understand your men are searching the grounds once more. May I ask what you're looking for?"

"I would think that's obvious."

"The murder weapon?"

He nodded.

"So it wasn't the hammer from the train room?"

"No, unfortunately. We got word from the lab that the hammer was not the object used."

"So you're back to square one."

He winced and said, "Yes, as you so nicely put it."

Then I suggested, "Just an idea of mine: It might not hurt to search for Mr. Moritz's metal cane."

"You mean, the old man who lives at the bottom of the hill?"

"Yes. He's been missing his cane since Monday."

"He didn't tell me that when I questioned him. How did you find out?"

"Oh, it just came up in conversation."

He eyed me intently and then remarked, "I guess there's a use for you after all. People might tell you things *in conversation* that they wouldn't necessarily convey to the police. I'll keep the cane in mind."

Then he asked, "Do you have any other tips for me?"

I reflected, and then said, "I'm just wondering, did Mrs. Schmied tell you about the stranger she saw?"

"She mentioned having seen an unfamiliar man walking down the hallway on the morning of the murder. So far, we haven't been able to put a face to that man. Do you have any suggestions as to that stranger?"

I shook my head, "Not yet."

"Thank you, Mrs. Huber. That is all for now."

As I got up to leave, he said, "Just a moment," and he jotted something down on his notepad. Then he tore the top paper off and handed it to me. I glanced at it. He had written a bunch of numbers with no name or explanation.

"Is this a phone number?"

"A direct line to me. If you learn more facts *in conversation*, call," he ordered.

Chapter 52

The following morning I sat on the veranda, sipping the last drop of coffee and taking a final puff from my cigarette. I hadn't smoked much on this trip and even less at Talblick, I mused. So I gave myself a pep talk: Against all odds, you might kick the nasty habit after all, old gal!

I was lost in thought when Helga appeared at the sliding-glass door.

She made me jump when she said, "Oh, there you are! Have you had breakfast?"

"Yes, I helped myself." And I said, "It's quiet. Where is everybody?"

She replied, "Alex took his family to Davos. I understand he has arrangements to make with the manager at the Sondereggli. Erika went to see the pastor, and Karl is probably still in bed."

"I see."

She volunteered, "We're expecting Norbert back today."

"Good. Where is Rex?"

"I believe he's in Mr. Sonderegger's bedroom."

"Has he eaten anything yet?"

"I don't think so."

"Where do you keep his dish?"

She looked at me with surprise and said, "You're planning to feed him?"

"I'll try."

She shrugged and uttered, "His food dish and water bowl is in the small utility room right off the entrance-hall. The cans of dog food are kept in the cabinet above the sink. Good luck!"

"Thanks, Helga. I'll make an attempt."

When I entered the bedroom, the German shepherd was sprawled out on the rug next to his dead master's bed. He raised his sad eyes up to me and then slowly got himself into a sitting position.

I ordered, "Come, Rex!" and started to walk back to the door. He just looked at me and didn't move.

"Come on, Rex! I know you're suffering, but you've got to make an effort."

I took a few more steps toward the hallway, and out of the corner of my eye I noticed him slowly getting to his feet and then following me.

"Good boy!"

In the utility room I glanced at the dish sitting on the floor. The food in it didn't look fresh. I commanded, "*Platz*, Rex!" He obediently sat down and watched me fill his drinking bowl with fresh water from the faucet. I sat the bowl down, and he lapped some up. Then he surveyed me while I dumped the old food, rinsed out the dish, opened a can and replenished his supply. I sat the meal in front of him, saying, "Eat, Rex! You need to keep up your strength."

He just stared at me.

"Well, I can wait." And since there was no chair in the room, I sat down next to him on the floor, stroking his fur and coaxing him toward the food. We spent a good twenty minutes together in the claustrophobic place, but he finally ate a few bites.

I praised, "Good, Rex! That'll do for the moment. We'll eat some more later. And now, let's go for a walk."

We hiked to the stream and back. Rex docilely trotted next to me, but his heart wasn't in it. He never wagged his tail, didn't jump into the water at the creek, and when I tossed a stick for him to retrieve, he didn't feel like playing.

As we strolled near the guest garage on our way back to the mansion, I said, "Come, Rex, let's see who's home!"

Alex's SUV was not there, but a silver BMW stood in one of the parking spaces.

"Looks like Norbert made it back!"

I could tell that the canine did not care one way or another.

Chapter 53

Norbert was nowhere to be found on the ground floor, so I went up to his room and knocked.

"Who is it?" I heard him say.

"It's Regula."

He opened the door and with a puzzled look on his face asked, "You've returned?"

"Didn't Erika tell you?"

"Except for Helga letting me in, I haven't seen a soul since I got here." And he continued in a whiny voice, "The funeral is tomorrow, so I came to help, and now I find no one home."

We were still standing in the doorframe, and I said, "I need to talk to you. May I come in?"

"Oh sure," and he stepped aside to let me enter.

His room had the same layout as the one I occupied, but, whereas the décor in mine was basically white, his was done in blue and beige.

He pointed at the small, square table and two chairs, asking, "Do you want to sit here, or shall we go out on the terrace?"

"I'd love to be outside."

When we were settled on the balcony, I explained the reason for my return to Talblick. As I did so, I kept my eyes on him. There was suffering showing in his face. His delicate features appeared strained, and the shadows below the eyes told of sleepless nights.

He remarked, "I didn't know you were a private investigator. How bizarre!" Then he blurted out, "The police already questioned me twice. I don't think I have the stomach to go through it once more."

"I'm sorry, Norbert, but I need to go over the events with you again." And I asked him about his movements on Monday.

His story tallied with the one I'd heard from Karl, except that he did not take a nap when getting to his room. Instead, he had made several last-minute business calls concerning the auction and then had applied himself to packing his bags. He had been unaware of the calamity that was taking place downstairs until Erika came to his room at about 15:30 conveying the terrible news.

"What happened next?" I inquired.

"I wanted to see for myself, but the police wouldn't let me into the train room. I was told to wait in the living room with everyone else. Later, the policemen searched the house, while at the same time their boss, Mr. Knupp, called us into Papa's office for questioning."

"So you saw your father last when he dropped in on you while having lunch?"

His pained expression deepened as he mumbled, "Yes," in a barely audible voice.

"I understand you made some unfortunate remarks after he left the kitchen."

Close to tears now, he said, "I'd give anything if I could take those words back. I've been haunted by them ever since I found out the exact circumstances of Papa's death."

I nodded.

He went on, "I didn't do it, Regula! But I feel guilty. I made that comment in anger, and then Papa gets killed in the exact way I threatened. It's almost as if I *willed* the murder. Oh, God help me, I feel so rotten!"

He broke down, slumping in his seat. I gave him time to collect himself and waited. Eventually, he pulled himself together, and I could see determination in his glance as he straightened up.

I felt it was best to change the subject and said, "So you left for Basel on Monday evening?"

"That's right. The auction was not until Wednesday, but Tuesday was a busy day with organizing and setting up for the event. At first, I was going to stay here and try to find someone who could manage the auction for me, but Erika urged me to go."

"I see."

He explained further, "I was one of the first persons to be questioned by Knupp, right after Erika and Alex. When he was through interviewing me, I told Erika it might be hard to find a replacement at such late notice. She insisted that I should go and manage the auction myself. She said it might do me good to get away."

"And was the event a success?"

"It went all right, but I couldn't concentrate. I kept thinking of Papa and of what I'd said at lunch. On top of that, Knupp came to question me once more early Wednesday morning, two hours before the auction started. When I'd talked to him on Monday, I didn't say anything about the lunch episode. By Wednesday, he knew and interrogated me in detail about it. Someone must have told on me. I was scared to death. I felt sure he'd come to arrest me."

"Well, he didn't," I stated. Then I suggested, "You look exhausted, try to get some rest," and I left him.

Chapter 54

As soon as I got to my room, I added more comments to my notes and then studied the list. I wished I had paid better attention to what people had told me the first time I was at the mansion. Somehow I felt what everyone had conveyed to me before the old man's death would be important. The first time around, they would not have been on their guard.

Then I descended the stairs, walked through the dining room and out onto the veranda. I went to the hammock, got comfortable in it, closed my eyes and resigned myself to serious brainwork.

Startled, I opened my eyes when Erika suddenly stood next to me, saying, "Are you asleep?" And she continued, "Evidently not, but you sure are jumpy! Want something to eat?"

"Lunchtime already?" I asked.

"It's past 1:00 in the afternoon," she replied. "How about sliced ham with melon?"

"Sounds delicious!"

"Go sit at the patio table and I'll bring it out," she said.

I must have lounged in the hammock for over an hour, I reflected. It had seemed like only minutes. Erika soon reappeared, carrying our food and drinks on a tray. We concentrated on eating and didn't speak.

Then she said, "Everything is settled with the church, so there's one less thing to worry about."

"Helga told me that Alex is making arrangements at the Sondereggli," I remarked. "I assume everyone will congregate there after the funeral?"

"Only Papa's business colleagues will go to the Sondereggli. Alex is making meal arrangements for those folks. Papa knew so many people that we decided to have two separate gatherings. The family and close friends will come up here after the church service. Helga is planning the meal for us. Most of it will be catered, though."

"Oh, I see."

Helga came out and handed Erika a letter, saying, "This just arrived via special delivery."

"Thank you," said Erika, and the housekeeper went back inside.

My friend looked at the letter, commenting, "It's addressed to all, but I'll open it," and she tore the seal.

I watched her as she read it, and soon a little smile came over her face. When she was done reading, she held on to the stationery sheets seemingly far away in thought. Then she handed the letter over and said, "It's from Maria. Go ahead and read it. I'd like you to get an idea of what a character my stepmother is."

I hesitated and questioned, "Are you sure you want me to read her letter?"

"Positive!"

The handwriting was large with a certain flair to it, suggesting self-assurance and independence in the writer. It read:

"Hello all!

"So Otto stepped on one toe too many and got himself killed.

"When I received Karl's message with the news, I was cruising along Glacier Bay. My first impulse was to abandon ship at the next port, hire a helicopter to get me to the nearest airport and take the fastest flights to Zurich. Now, an hour later, I've changed my mind.

"I can say good-bye to Otto from any corner of the globe. What good is a funeral, after all? I cherish the wonderful years I spent with your father. Some of you (maybe all of you) might reproach me for having left so suddenly. I needed more space. Had I stayed, resentment on my part would have been unavoidable, followed by quarrels between Otto and me. This way, we both had good memories. I remained his 'Gypsy bride' forever.

"I have a consolation for you all. Your father lived his life by taking risks and never shied away from the consequences. I'm not only referring to the risks he took in business matters and with his sports activities. I gather he went quickly and painlessly. The old man would have hated to die in a hospital or in his own bed at the end of a prolonged illness.

"I'll be thinking about you all at Talblick on Saturday, and I'll raise my glass in a special toast to Otto!

"Love, Maria."

I looked at my friend and said, "She definitely seems a free spirit."

She nodded. Then she remarked, "I don't think I'll show the letter to Norbert. He might take offense. As for the rest of us, I'm sure her lines are a comfort."

Following a long period of silence I asked, "May I borrow your car this afternoon?"

"Surely. I don't need it anymore today. Where are you going?"

"Another visit to Mr. Moritz is indicated," I replied.

Chapter 55

I decided not to hike to Dörfli for a couple of reasons. I had already engaged in a little exercise earlier when taking Rex for a walk, and more importantly, I did not want to take the chance of discomfort should I again be offered cider. I was getting the feel for the narrow, twisting road. After driving around the first few bends, I could anticipate the exact location of the next curve. I got cocky and said to myself, I dare you, Alex, to drive up from the opposite direction with your big SUV!

When I arrived at my destination, I didn't have to worry about being offered any cider. On the contrary, I came face to face with a hostile Mr. Moritz.

The old gentleman opened the door and exclaimed, "You again! You've got a nerve to come back."

Astonished, I asked, "What did I do?"

"Don't act as if you didn't know!"

"Oh, did the police pay you another visit?"

This seemed to infuriate him even more, and he went on, "A visit? Interrogation and house search is what they did to me!" And he continued, "I thought you liked me, but I was wrong! You blabbed to Herr Knupp and sent him on my tail."

"Let's go sit down and talk this over, Mr. Moritz."

He was about to shut the door in my face but seemed to have a change of heart, saying, "Come in, then."

He limped to the living room, and I trailed behind him. When seated, I said, "In a murder investigation, we have to cooperate with the police and - -"

He interrupted, "What has telling them about my missing cane got to do with cooperation?"

"The murder weapon has not been found yet," I replied.

"You think my cane was the murder weapon?"

"Not necessarily."

"Not necessarily," he mimicked, as his anger was soaring again. "I certainly didn't hit Otto over the head with it. I told Knupp as much."

I asked, "Do you mind telling me about this morning's interview?"

He shrugged and said, "Why not? I've got nothing to hide. Herr Knupp questioned me while two other police officers searched my house and yard. He told me he'd heard that I was missing my metal cane since Monday." Sarcastically, he added, "I wonder where he heard that! Knupp wanted me to tell him when I had last seen my cane, et cetera, et cetera.

"Here is what I told him and am telling you now: I'm pretty sure I had the cane when I drove up to Otto's house. I think I had it when I went inside. After that, I'm not sure anymore. It had stopped raining for just a few minutes when I got to the mansion, but I took my umbrella along, since it looked like it would start again at any moment. Sure enough, when I left, it was pouring cats and dogs again."

He continued, "When I woke up from a nap that afternoon, I missed the cane, and I first searched the car and then the house. I supposed that I might have dropped it next to my car in front of the mansion while fighting to get the umbrella closed as I got into the driver's seat. I'm not positive about that, but at the time I thought it might have happened that way. Anyhow, I decided not to worry about it for the time being and that I would call Otto's house the next day asking if anyone had found the cane there."

"I see."

He went on, "Before I got around to calling the next morning, the police showed up and told me the bad news. I was shocked, of course, and forgot all about the cane. Besides, it would've been in poor taste to call at a house of mourning inquiring about the whereabouts of my stupid stick."

"Yes, I can understand that," I said.

The little old gentleman seemed irate as he continued, "The police found the cane in my backyard, and instead of handing it over, they dropped it into one of their plastic bags and left. Mr. Knupp had the nerve to tell me they needed to 'borrow' it. Then he questioned me some more about the damned walking stick. I told him that I had no idea how it got into my backyard. I said that I might be old, but that didn't automatically make me an idiot. Even a senile fellow wouldn't go for a stroll around his yard in the pouring rain and drop the thing behind a bush."

I chuckled and said, "You're definitely not senile, Mr. Moritz!"

"Not yet," he retorted, seemingly getting his good humor back.

"Actually, I didn't come to talk about the cane. I'd like to inquire about something entirely different."

"Glad to hear it. I'm sick and tired of discussing the cane. I wish I had it to walk on instead."

"When you waited in the entrance-hall at Talblick on Monday, did you see anyone besides Helga when she let you in?"

"I saw the masseur fellow go into the laundry room with an armful of dirty towels. A second later he came back out mumbling, 'Oh, someone is washing sheets. I'll have to wait,' and carried his load back out again. Then he nodded at me and went down the corridor."

I asked, "Did you come across anyone else?"

"No, I didn't."

"Did you see Laura Thompson, for instance, or anyone of the family?"

"I told you, no!"

"That's all I wanted to know. Thanks for talking to me." And giving him my best smile, I asked, "Can you forgive me about the cane business?"

"I'll think about it," he replied with just a hint of a twinkle in his eye.

Chapter 56

Peter called that Friday night telling me all about the neat things he'd been doing while staying in my hometown. He even took advantage of the warm weather and went swimming at the *Tiefenbrunnen* beach in Lake Zurich.

I asked, "What's next on your itinerary?"

"I might head for Lucerne, then maybe Interlaken and Grindelwald to do the tourist thing."

"Have a great time!"

Then he inquired, "How is your case coming along?"

"I've accumulated so much info, it makes my head spin!"

"Want to unburden yourself?"

"I thought you'd never ask. Do you have a couple of hours?"

He laughed and said, "That bad, huh? Shoot, I've got all night."

So I proceeded to "unburden" myself as he suggested. I repeated what each person had conveyed to me in his or her interview, leaving nothing out. Peter is a good listener, and he patiently waited till the end of my narrative.

Then he commented, "You've got tons of information there. All you have to do is separate facts from fiction!"

"Precisely."

He remarked, "The most obvious suspect is Norbert, of course."

"So that's how it strikes you?"

"You don't agree?"

"Think about it, Peter. Norbert makes the comment at lunch that he'd like to see his father drowned in the miniature lake. Then, three hours later, Otto Sonderegger gets murdered in exactly that way!"

"You can't possibly think that was coincidental."

"Certainly not!"

"Oh, I get it! You figure Norbert planted the idea in someone else's head with his remark."

"Voilà!"

"So all you have to do is take the people who were having lunch with Norbert under scrutiny. If I'm not mistaken, you said that would be Erika and Alex with wife and daughter. Oh, and the other son, Karl, who apparently joined them just as his brother made that unfortunate statement."

"It's not that simple," I declared. "Everyone else concerned could have overheard Norbert's remark."

"Explain that to me."

"Okay. Helga could have heard from the entrance-hall or the dining room. Laura Thompson got to the mansion shortly before noon, so she was in the house at the right time. Hans Weber was passing in and out of the laundry room, which is right next to the entrance-hall. Rita Schmied, the cleaning woman, was all over the place dusting and vacuuming. Fritz Moritz told me he left the residence before Otto Sonderegger came out of the kitchen. If he was truthful, he had already walked out of the house when Norbert uttered that remark."

He questioned, "You think Moritz might have been lying and actually talked to Otto Sonderegger?"

"No, that's not what I meant. Mr. Moritz could have hidden in either the utility or the laundry room when Otto Sonderegger came out of the kitchen. Then, after his friend disappeared down the corridor he could have stationed himself in the entrance-hall once more."

"All right, Regula! You've made your point." And he added, "I also gathered from what you've told me about the interviews that most of these people had an opportunity to sneak into the train room around 3:00 p.m. and do the dirty deed."

"Not just most of them, all of them," I corrected.

"Surely, you can eliminate the masseur and the old guy. Neither one of them was at the mansion at 3:00."

I stated, "Hans Weber claimed he left at approximately 2:15 p.m., but that is not a proven fact, as yet. The same goes for Mr. Moritz. He might have been there at the time of the murder."

"Come now, don't tell me the old gentleman was hiding in the mansion for three hours. That makes no sense whatsoever!"

"No, but he could've come back."

Peter argued, "I'm certain the housekeeper would've told you if she'd admitted him a second time!"

"True, but he was a regular guest at the mansion and must have known that the door to the veranda was never kept locked during the day."

After a pause, he said, "So I guess you have to concentrate on motive. I've recently read someplace that aside from street crimes, gang-related matters, and serial killings, there are basically three types of motives for murder: number one, greed; number two, passion; and number three, self-preservation."

"You're quite the scholar," I teased.

Ignoring my remark, he continued, "I would presume Otto Sonderegger's murder falls into the category of greed."

"You might be right."

He kept going, "The three sons as well as the court reporter clearly have a motive. You can also include Alex's wife and daughter. As for the rest, I can't see that they'd have one. Going by the motive angle, then, you can eliminate lots of individuals as suspects."

I said, "Plenty of others had a possible reason for killing Mr. Sonderegger. There are only two people I can't tag with a plausible motive, but that doesn't mean that they didn't have one!"

"Don't tell me you even suspect your friend!"

"I have to be objective. I can't leave Erika out of the picture, nor her boyfriend, for that matter."

"I forgot about him." Then he said, "The Claude person clearly couldn't have overheard Norbert at lunch. Didn't you say he dropped Erika off at around 9:30 in the morning?"

"You've paid attention! Erika could have phoned, telling him about Norbert's comment. He also could've orientated himself about the entrance to the house from the veranda while he was looking over the tennis court."

Then he asked, "What do you think of this stranger that the cleaning lady told you about? Do you believe he exists, or did she make him up?"

"The stranger story is interesting, isn't it? I believe Mrs. Schmied saw a man walking down the hallway. Whether or not he was a stranger, I haven't figured out yet."

"What do you mean?"

"In my opinion Rita Schmied did hear fragments of conversation coming out of Sonderegger's office while she was next door cleaning his bedroom. I don't think she has such a vivid imagination as to have made that up. So it follows that she associated the man walking down the corridor with the person talking to her employer a few minutes earlier. The only thing I'm not clear about is whether this man was someone she had never seen before or if she was lying and knew him well."

Peter sounded surprised when he said, "Why would she lie about that?"

"Maybe it was someone she wanted to protect."

"I get you."

I continued, "Stranger or not, according to Claude Boreau, there was a man hiking down from Talblick to Dörfli at approximately 9:45 on Monday morning."

"Which confirms the cleaning lady's story," Peter said.

"True, but Boreau could've been the stranger himself and might have made the hiker up."

"Why would he?"

"I know that Erika's boyfriend has a quick and sharp mind. Let's pretend for a moment that he is the villain. I questioned him about having seen anyone by car or on foot on his drive down from Talblick. He had to assume that I had good reason to ask that question. So he figured that someone might have caught a glimpse of him while he was at the mansion that morning. He promptly makes up the hiker and cleverly mentions that at the time he thought it was odd to come across some man trekking about on a rainy day. He also stated that he didn't get a close look at the man, but that the fellow was tall. He even was precise on where he'd spotted the hiker, namely at the bottom of the hill close to Dörfli.

"So you see, he covered himself on two accounts. Claude is of medium height. Letting me know that he saw the man practically at the end of the guy's hike down gave him a better alibi time."

"I've lost you about alibi time."

I explained, "Boreau was vague about the time he dropped Erika off. He said it might have been before 9:30 a.m. Then in reply to my question about how long he'd been on the grounds checking out the tennis court, he said ten to fifteen minutes. So that would put the time when he saw the hiker at roughly 9:45 a.m."

"I still don't get it!"

"According to the cleaning woman she overheard the fragments of conversation in Sonderegger's office at approximately 9:00 a.m. In her words, 'a little later,' she saw the stranger walk away. Even though Mrs. Schmied was not precise about the time, 'a little later' is definitely not thirty to forty minutes. So if Claude was the perpetrator, he made sure the timing of his presence on the Talblick estate would be taken as much later."

"Got you now! So you suspect the boyfriend?"

"Not at all. I just wanted to point out that he could possibly be the 'stranger.'"

"What about this business of the old man's cane? Do you think he dropped it in his own backyard, or do you feel it's more likely that someone was trying to frame him?"

"I'm not speculating about that yet. We won't know if the cane was the murder weapon until the police have examined it."

After a pause he questioned, "Is there another exit out of the train room besides the one to the hallway?"

"No. What do you have in mind?"

"Just wondering why the dog would have let the murderer leave."

"I thought about that too. I came to the conclusion that the storm was an excellent ally for the killer."

"What has the storm got to do with it?"

"According to Ernst Knupp of the police, the trains first had a free run after Mr. Sonderegger let go of the controls. Then came the big crash. I envision that the murderer left the room during the short time of the trains still running on their own. The killer closed the door behind him or her, telling Rex '*Platz*' in passing. If there was an outcry from Mr. Sonderegger or a noise when the trains crashed moments later, a blast of thunder might have drowned all that out. The dog's reaction would've been delayed by hearing the sounds of the storm, and therefore he started barking after the fact."

"Yes. I guess that makes sense."

There was a pause in the line, and then Peter chuckled and said, "Well, what I've learned from this long discussion of ours is this: You can eliminate Norbert as a suspect!"

"I disagree."

"What? Weren't we in accord that he wouldn't blurt out his intention of drowning his dad and then go ahead and commit the murder in that fashion?"

"Yes, but Norbert could've been clever! He'd figure that the police would come to that conclusion and might be looking for a suspect among the people who'd overheard his remark."

"Stop! You're giving me a headache!"

I laughed and said, "I'm glad we had this chat. Mulling over a case with you always helps me getting a better perspective."

Then he asked, "When is the funeral?"

"Tomorrow."

"Want me to come?"

"Thanks for offering, but go ahead and do your 'tourist thing'!"

Chapter 57

After the funeral service held at a church in Davos, I rode back to Talblick with Helga. When we came out of the church, the old housekeeper had seemed near emotional collapse. I offered to take the wheel, but she said, "Don't be silly. This is my car, and I'm certainly capable of driving it." Once on the road, I made an attempt at conversation, but she was understandably not in a talkative mood. The silence between us gave me ample time to reminisce about the day's developments up to that point.

After breakfast I meant to take Rex for a short stroll before getting myself ready to attend the funeral, since a chance of rain was predicted for later in the day. As it turned out, I never got around to taking that walk. I peeked into the late Sonderegger's bedroom, but Rex wasn't there. When I went by the dictating room, I noticed the door to it was closed. That's almost eerie, I thought to myself. I've always found it open before. As I walked past the room, I heard a sound coming from within. I considered it possible that Rex might be locked up inside, so I opened the door and entered.

To my astonishment I found Laura there instead. An empty box stood on top of the desk and all the drawers were pulled open. With a touch of sadness I glanced at the upholstered chair. Except for the young woman's raincoat draped over the armrest, the dictating chair was ominously vacant. She looked at me, and I noticed that her eyes were moist.

I said, "I'm sorry! I heard a noise and thought I might find Rex in here. I don't want to disturb you."

"That's all right. Come on in."

I took a few steps inside but left the door open.

She explained, "I came up before the funeral to clear out and pack my things." And motioning at the box, she remarked, "As you can see, I haven't gotten far. I needed to say good-bye to Mr. Sonderegger first."

"I understand."

"I'd better get on with it," and she started to take things out of the drawers. Then she pointed at a big pile of papers neatly stacked on the nearby shelf and asked, "What shall I do with the unfinished manuscript?" And she went on sadly, "I doubt anyone would want to take up where he left off and complete it."

"Keep it in a safe place. The police might be interested in taking a look."

"Do you really think so?" Then she contemplated, "I imagine the memoirs would help them to learn about Mr. Sonderegger's past."

I nodded. Then with a gesture encircling the room I said, "Must be hard for you to come in here and pack your belongings."

"It sure is." Then she said, "On Monday I'll turn the car in to the leasing company. Mrs. Graff said I could keep it as long as I want, but I really won't need it in Davos. I can walk just about anywhere I'd care to go." With a sigh she remarked, "I'm anxious to go home now."

Then she motioned to her steno-machine still sitting on the tripod, saying regretfully, "I'll have to set this up at lawyers' offices again soon."

"Have you booked a flight yet?"

"Yes, for next Thursday. I hope I don't have to cancel it. I haven't cleared it with the police yet. I'm keeping my fingers crossed that Mr. Knupp doesn't want me to stick around if the homicide isn't solved by then."

I stated, "I trust the case will be cracked soon. My husband and I are flying back on Thursday too. What airline did you book your flight with? Swiss?"

"Sure did."

"We'll be on the same plane, then. Well, I'll leave you to do your packing. Will I see you later?"

"Of course, I'll see you at the funeral. My aunt and uncle are coming too. I'll introduce you."

"I'd love to meet them," I replied and left her to her task.

Coming back to the present, I looked over at Helga in the driver's seat. She kept her eyes focused on the road, and I didn't like the stolid expression on her face. Again, I was reminded of how hard this tragedy had hit her.

Then I reverted back to my musing. The church had been packed, not only with family and friends, but a great number of business associates, I presumed. Helga and I found seats close to the center aisle halfway down the nave. As the family of the deceased passed by on their way to the first pews, I noticed a handsome man walking next to Norbert. Must be his partner, I guessed. Claude was not with Erika. I spotted him at the back of the church as people were leaving at the conclusion of the service. The man in uniform making his way down the aisle with the Alex Sonderegger family was obviously Alex's son. When he was even with me I got a good look at him. He resembled Otto Sonderegger strongly. The young man was extremely tall and carried himself in the same way his grandfather used to. He had a full head of hair, light eyes and the same stubbornly pointed chin. Apparently the grandson took after his grandpa with his looks more than did any of the sons. Where had I recently seen a similar chin, I wondered?

I had spotted other familiar faces in the congregation. Fritz Moritz was there, looking frail. Hans Weber was seated a couple of pews in front of us, and though he never turned his head, I recognized the blond giant clearly from the back. I located Rita Schmied with presumably her husband across the aisle from us. Ernst Knupp had been standing near the church entrance and I was curious as to why he attended the funeral. Was it possible he wanted to check out the mourners?

I didn't see Laura Thompson and her relatives, but they must have been sitting somewhere behind us, I deduced. As soon as I could get a chance with Laura alone, I needed to ask her a question. Seconds before the service started, Karl rushed by, hurrying to his seat in the front. Had he really overslept on the day of his father's funeral? Incredible!

As we were driving through Dörfli, I perceived guiltily that I hadn't paid much attention to the service. Rather, I had mulled over the possible murder suspects. Forgive me, Mr. Sonderegger, I pondered. I'll remember you during the next full moon!

Helga ended my meditating by stopping the car in front of the mansion, saying, "The caterers are already waiting. I'd better hurry and let them in."

Chapter 58

Roughly 40 to 50 people had gathered at Talblick. Just family and close friends, it appeared. At a glance, I didn't see many folks older than sixty; these people would most likely be friends of Erika and her brothers. I imagined that a good many of Otto Sonderegger's contemporaries had predeceased him, as my own parents had. Judging by the crowd I had observed at the church, a large group had been his business acquaintances and would now meet at the Sondereggli.

While some of the caterers were setting up a large buffet in the dining room, others passed around drinks and appetizers. I was talking to a guest out on the veranda when a young lady offered me goodies from a tray. So Helga had found a use for the Appenzeller cheese, I noticed.

I was on my way to the bathroom and looked into Sonderegger's bedroom. Rex was back on his rug, and I stopped in for a minute.

I petted the dog and said, "You finally ventured out of this room earlier. Good for you!"

He just glanced at me ruefully.

I promised, "Later, when all the people have left, we'll go for a walk!"

He didn't look enthusiastic about the prospect.

Don't forget to ask Laura that question, I told myself as I climbed the stairs to my room. A few minutes later I mingled with the guests once more. People were starting to fill their plates and then either sat in the dining room or carried their food to the living room. Some walked out to the veranda and found seats there. I wasn't hungry but dutifully helped myself to a few treats and carried my plate outside. The weatherman had obviously been wrong in his prediction, for I couldn't detect a single rain cloud in the sky. Lotti was sitting on the hammock alone.

I drifted in her direction and said, "Scoot over. There's room for two."

The girl moved aside a little but did not respond. She wore a sullen expression on her face and obviously hadn't touched the tiny bit of food on her plate. She eyed the guests around us with distaste.

I said, "I sympathize with you. I'm not particularly hungry either."

She still kept silent, and I didn't urge her to talk. We sat quietly as I surveyed the folks mingling on the patio.

All of a sudden, the teenager blurted out, "Opa was murdered and we just buried him. Look at all these people stuffing themselves and acting as if this was a party. It's disgusting!"

"I understand that you feel that way, but it's customary to share a meal with family and friends after a funeral."

She jumped to her feet and said, "Maybe, but I can't stand it anymore. I'm going to my room."

I watched her running away, barely avoiding a collision with an elderly person as she made for the sliding-glass door. At her age I'd probably feel the same way, I reflected.

When finished eating, I picked up the plate Lotti had dropped on the grass and went inside as well. I deposited the dishes and silverware in the kitchen. Helga was giving the catering personnel directions for serving coffee and dessert. Then I walked into the dining room where people gathered in little groups. Erika was talking to a couple in their mid-forties. I didn't want to intrude, so I passed by them and strolled to the living room, where most people seemed to have gathered. I spotted Mr. Moritz deep in conversation with another man. Alex and Mirella introduced me to their son. We exchanged pleasantries about his military training, but my heart wasn't in it. A persisting uneasiness lurked in the back of my mind. I finally excused myself and went out to the hallway. Erika came from the opposite direction, carrying a few dishes to the kitchen.

I stopped her and inquired, "Have you seen Laura?"

"No, but her aunt and uncle just asked me the same thing. Apparently they'd missed each other at the service."

I tried not to show my anxiety as I said, "Never mind. I'll find her."

By that time I was really worried. Obviously, I hadn't been the only one who didn't see her at the funeral. Her relatives had missed her too. And now she apparently wasn't among the guests in either room, nor out on the patio. Quickening my step I walked the length of the corridor and opened the door to the family room. Except for the furniture it was empty. I glanced briefly into the train room. The trains still lay derailed, but there was no one there. I checked all the downstairs bathrooms with the same result. I stuck my head in Sonderegger's bedroom. Rex had not moved from the rug. Then I bypassed his office as well as the massage room and headed for the dictating room.

Chapter 59

I opened the door and entered. An involuntary shriek escaped me as I came upon the ghastly scene. The tripod was lying on the floor and Laura was sort of propped up against it in a half sitting, half reposing position. A transparent shopping bag was pulled over her head, its strings tied tightly around her neck. I came a few steps closer. Her eyes stared unseeing beneath the plastic. She had obviously died of suffocation and was long beyond help. Still, I had to fight the urge to free her from the bag, but knew better than to touch anything. I glanced at the desk immediately behind her. The box still stood on top of it, now halfway filled with some of her possessions. Next to the box sat her steno-machine and laptop. I quickly surveyed the rest of the room. Nothing appeared changed since I had last seen it a few hours earlier. Laura's coat still lay on the armrest of the upholstered chair, and the memoir manuscript pages on the shelf appeared untouched. I automatically looked at my watch. It was 2:07 p.m.

I pulled myself together and thought of a quick plan of action. Then I went out of the room, shutting the door behind me. I ran to the late Mr. Sonderegger's bedroom three doors down the hall and stood in the doorway.

I ordered, "Rex! *Fuss!* Come quickly."

The German shepherd followed me back down the corridor, if not quickly, at least obediently. When we got to the dictating room, I had him sit in front of the closed door.

I gave the command, "*Platz!* Don't let anyone enter the room. I'm counting on you, Rex!"

Then I ran along the hallway and up the stairs to my room, grabbed my cell phone and hurried back to Rex. Although I could hear folks talking in the living and dining room, I didn't encounter anybody on my mission.

When I got back, I said, "Good dog!" and made my call to Ernst Knupp's direct line.

Then I saw a guest down the hall coming out of the bathroom next to the living room.

I yelled, "Sir!"

He looked my way and I motioned him to come. He hesitated at first, but when I waved again, he walked down the corridor toward me, staring at me and then at Rex.

I asked, "Do you know Mrs. Graff?"

"Erika? Of course I know her," he replied, perplexed.

"Please seek her out and tell her to come to the dictating room right away."

The man clearly thought I was a halfwit and repeated, "The *dictating* room?"

"Yes, please hurry!"

"And to whom do I have the pleasure of speaking?"

Just my luck I had to deal with someone that liked to chat, I thought.

Aloud, I said, "R.A. Huber," without bothering to ask for his name.

He got the hint and said, "So I am to find Erika and tell her to meet R.A. Huber in the dictating room?"

"Please! It's urgent."

He finally turned around, and I saw him shaking his head as he walked quickly back to the living room.

Soon Erika hurried down the hall. I told her to brace herself for another tragedy and then informed her of what I had discovered behind the closed door.

She gasped and exclaimed, "Oh no! What kind of a monster do we have among us?"

I let her collect herself and then asked, "Are her aunt and uncle still here?"

"Oh my God! I'll have to face them and tell them what happened." Then she said, "I guess I'll call the police first and then break the horrible news to Laura's relatives."

"You don't have to call the authorities. I already did."

Chapter 60

The following Monday I was sitting on my room terrace, waiting to be called for questioning once more. It had already turned evening when the police finished with the murder scene on Saturday. Then Mr. Knupp questioned me first, since I'd found the body. After my statement, he interviewed the guests, one by one. Plenty of food was left over from the luncheon, so no one had to go hungry. The time was close to 10:00 p.m. when the last visitor finally left. So the police chief informed us that he'd take the household members' statements on Monday and that he expected everyone to be available for questioning at 9:00 sharp that morning.

Sunday dragged on. The morale at Talblick was understandably at an extreme low. Everyone was at last facing the truth that we had a ruthless killer in our midst. When I went to breakfast, I found Erika at the kitchen counter trying to force down a piece of toast. She seemed utterly dejected and miserable.

She had looked at me pleadingly, exclaiming, "You've got to help us, Regula! Find out who's committing these horrendous crimes."

"I'm working on it. Bear with me, please!"

As tears started to run down her cheeks, she said, "After I'd recuperated from the loss of Robert and Stefan, I thought that the experience had made me strong and I'd be able to handle anything life would bring my way. I was wrong. I can't cope with what happened now."

In the afternoon I had taken Rex for a long walk, trying to sort things out in my mind. Then I sat in my room going over the notes I had made when interviewing each person. I wished I had jotted things down during my first visit. But then, how could I? At the time I had no inkling that I would eventually have to solve two murders. Now, I had to rely solely on my memory. I pondered each conversation I had with every person, including Otto Sonderegger himself, from that Wednesday when I first arrived at Talblick until I left Sunday, exactly a week ago. I tried to remember each dialogue and event in the correct order, and then compared the statements the suspects had made after Sonderegger's murder, looking for discrepancies.

The process was tedious, but when I sat on the balcony of my room on Monday, I started to connect the dots and knew I was finally headed in the right direction. Whether or not I was ever going to prove any of it was a different matter.

I was abruptly taken out of my thought process when there was a knock at the door, and Helga stuck her head in, saying, "Herr Knupp is ready for you."

I looked at my watch. It was 4:00 in the afternoon already. I must have sat there for hours!

"I'm coming," I said and followed her downstairs.

Chapter 61

As soon as I faced the officer, he came straight to the point. "You've given me your statement about finding Laura Thompson's body on Saturday already. I'd like to verify a couple of facts, however."

He looked at his record and then asked, "What time do you have?"

I glanced at my wristwatch and answered, "4:03 p.m. I mean 16:03."

He checked his own watch, and stated, "Correct."

"Why are we synchronizing our watches?"

"You discovered the victim's body at 14:07 on Saturday. Are you sure you're right about that time?"

"Yes, I checked my watch a few seconds after entering the dictating room."

He looked down at his notes again and then stated, "Amazing! Your call to my direct line came through at 14:11."

"I'm at a loss what you're driving at," I said.

He read from my statement, quoting, "I went out of the room, shutting the door. I ran to the late Mr. Sonderegger's bedroom and ordered Rex, the dog, to come with me. I had him sit in front of the dictating room, ordering him to stay put and not let anyone enter. Then I ran to my room, grabbed the phone and hurried back. When I returned, Rex still sat there, and I called you."

I stared at him. I had absolutely no idea what was on his mind.

He managed a smile, saying "You ran three doors down the hall to get the dog and placed him in front of the victim's door. Then you ran three-fourths of the corridor, up the stairs, four doors away to your bedroom, grabbed the phone and I presume the piece of paper with my phone number written on it, made your way back down the stairs, ran along the long hall again, and then stopped by the door of the crime scene where you made the call to me. All this in four minutes. You're some sprinter!"

"You've done your homework and checked out where my room is located." Then I got serious and said, "I can run fast if I need to. I didn't have to search for your phone number, by the way. I programmed it into the phone on the day you gave it to me."

He nodded. The expression on his face became grave as he continued, "In the meantime I've taken everyone else's statement. It looks like you were the last person to see Laura Thompson alive." He consulted his records and said, "Let's go over the events of Saturday morning once more. Please tell me again what you did from about 9:00 onward."

I complied, "I had breakfast around 8:50. Then at 9:10 or so, I talked to Laura Thompson in the dictating room. She was in the process of packing her things into a box. I chatted with her a few minutes, ten at most. When I passed the kitchen on my way to the stairs leading up to my room, Helga Hodler stopped me, calling through the open door. She suggested that I ride to the funeral with her. She was setting out some dishes and serving platters on the counter, presumably getting ready for the guests after the funeral service. She told me that she would soon be done with the preparations but still needed to change her clothes. I replied that I was going up to change as well. She said that we should leave at 9:45 in order to get there before the family so we'd find a good seat in the church. As you know, the service started at 10:30."

I stopped my narrative, but he still looked at me attentively, as if he expected me to go on.

So I continued, "Helga was true to her word and knocked at my door at 9:45, ready to go. She also gave me a ride back after the funeral. We got to Talblick shortly after 12:00. The caterers were already waiting in front of the mansion for the housekeeper to let them in."

He said, "Yes, that's clear."

I had already told him all this on Saturday and was sure he'd been looking for discrepancies in my two statements.

He went on with his questioning, "Why did you seek Laura Thompson out in the morning?"

"I was looking for the dog."

He raised an eyebrow and said, "In that room?"

I explained how I'd wanted to take Rex for a walk and couldn't find him and how, when I'd heard a noise coming from the dictating room, I thought it was possible Rex had been locked in there. When making this remark, I was aware that it might have sounded fishy to the police officer.

He seemed to take my statement at face value, however, and said, "I can see you're taking an interest in that dog."

"Someone has to," I answered.

Then I said, "So I was the last person to talk to Laura and also the one who found her body hours later. Does that make me your prime suspect?"

He appeared amused and said, "There is the question of motive, and I cannot come up with one as far as you're concerned. In every case I allow for one coincidence. In this double murder, the coincidence seems to be that you and the young woman victim came from roughly the same area."

My home in Merida and my office in Pasadena are a far stretch from Balboa Island, but I could understand the remark from his point of view.

He went on, "I cannot put you anywhere near the murder scene of Otto Sonderegger, and the two crimes are obviously connected."

"I'm cleared of suspicion, then?"

"I wouldn't go as far as that. I have to keep an open mind."

"Of course."

"Getting back to Saturday morning, what did you and Laura Thompson talk about?"

"Oh, just about her plans in the near future. She was anxious to get home."

Then he said, "When I first talked to you on Saturday, you told me that you'd become uneasy when you didn't see her among the guests and that you searched the ground floor and consequently found her body."

"Yes, that is so."

"Why were you looking for her in the first place?"

"I needed an answer to a question I forgot to ask during my interview with her in Davos."

"What was the question?"

"It had to do with the last few chapters in the manuscript of the memoirs." And I added, "That reminds me, did you confiscate the manuscript? When I talked to Laura on Saturday morning it was sitting on a shelf in the dictating room. I noticed that the manuscript pages were still there later when I found her body, but after your people were done with the room, it was gone."

He replied, "I wouldn't call it 'confiscating'. We collected it for evidence. I spent a good part of my Sunday reading the entire 29 chapters. It made for an interesting read. The old man was apparently a character.

I didn't come across anything that might help us in our investigation, however."

Surprised, I asked, "Did you say 29 chapters? Are you sure about that number?"

"Positive," he said, appearing slightly irritated.

"In that case there are a few chapters missing."

Astounded, he said, "You read it?"

"No, but I happen to know that there were more than 29 chapters in that transcript."

"Explain yourself, please."

"I met Laura Thompson the day after I came to Talblick on my first visit.   That would've been on Thursday before Otto Sonderegger's murder. On that occasion she explained her work to me and in conversation mentioned that her boss had dictated 31 chapters up to that point. Then, when I talked to her more recently in Davos, she told me that on Friday before the tragedy, Mr. Sonderegger had dictated for hours. In fact, he'd added three more chapters to the memoirs, so the manuscript should have a total of 34 chapters."

He remarked, "It's astounding the information you seem to be able to amass in conversation! What do you think happened to chapters 30 through 34?"

"A good guess would be that the murderer took them and possibly destroyed them."

He agreed, "There could have been incriminating information in those chapters. When we examined the crime scene, we couldn't find a backup disc. If there was one, the killer must have taken that too. It's probably useless to check Thompson's laptop. I'm sure those chapters would've been deleted as well, but we'll check anyhow."

I smiled and said, "You're in luck as far as the backup disc is concerned. I know that Laura kept it at her aunt's house in Davos. I think the court reporter was conscientious enough to have taken the disc home on that tragic day, despite being upset."

"You found that out 'in conversation' too," he observed. "I'll give her relatives a call as soon as I'm through with you. If the disc is at their house, they'd better put it under lock and key."

Then he went on, "Is there any other information you can give me regarding either of the murders?"

"I can't think of anything else at the moment," I answered, "but may I ask you a few things?"

"I might not tell you, but go ahead."

"Was Mr. Moritz's cane the murder weapon in the first crime?"

"Yes, that is established."

Then I said, "I didn't want to pester my friend Erika with this. Did you talk with the estate lawyers?"

"But you have no scruples pestering me! We won't know about the will for another week. The lawyer firm is having *Betriebsferien* at the moment."

"Oh, that's right. Some businesses in Europe close shop while everyone goes on vacation. I've lived in the States so long that I've forgotten." And I commented, "I don't think who benefits according to the will is crucial to us anyhow. Much more important is whom each person *believed* the will would benefit."

"Exactly."

"I have questions about the second murder too," I said.

"I thought you might!"

"Was Laura knocked unconscious with her own tripod before the plastic bag was pulled over her head to suffocate her?"

"It appears that way, but I haven't got the lab report on the tripod as yet. Is that all?"

"One more thing, please! Has Laura Thompson's time of death been established?"

He hesitated and then said, "What the heck, there's no harm in telling you. The medical examiner tended to the corpse at 14:35. He estimated the time of death between four and six hours prior to that time."

I quickly did some calculating and deduced, "I saw her alive at 9:20, so she was killed between 9:20 and 10:35."

He nodded.

I mumbled, more to myself than to him, "More likely between 9:20 and 10:05 since everyone was at the funeral by 10:30."

He asked ironically, "Are we through now, lady detective?"

I smiled and got up. Halfway to the door I turned around and said, "May I ask you something personal?"

"What now?"

"Was Otto Sonderegger a friend of yours?"

"No. What gives you that idea?"

"I was just wondering why you attended his funeral?"

Keeping a straight face he answered, "I was curious about any 'strange' mourners. As it turned out, it was a good thing I showed up and saw who came running in at the last minute!"

Chapter 62

When Peter called that evening I told him about the latest murder. As always, he paid attention while I explained every detail.

Then he said, "At least you can cross one suspect off your list."

"Don't joke about this, Peter. I liked Laura Thompson a great deal. It's a tragedy that her young life ended in such a brutal way."

"Of course, and I wasn't making fun of the situation. I simply meant that you have one less suspect to worry about."

"True."

Then he asked, "Do you think one of the sons killed her assuming that with her gone, his father's will would revert back to its original state?"

"That's a possibility," I replied.

"But you have something different in mind?"

"Well, with those last chapters of the memoirs missing, I tend to think that whether she herself was aware of it or not, Laura Thompson must have known something incriminating to the murderer."

"Yes, that makes sense." Then he said, "I get the feeling you've figured it all out. Am I right?"

"You read me like a book! I think I'm on the right track, but I can't prove anything as yet."

"Why don't you take Knupp into your confidence? He sounds pretty sharp."

"There's nothing he could do at this point without proof. I've got to figure out how to get some evidence, and then I'll tell him. Besides, I might be wrong."

After a pause I said, "I'm pretty sure I won't miss our flight on Thursday."

He exclaimed, "I don't give a damn about that! You can always take a later flight, if necessary. I'm worried about your safety."

"Oh."

"Yes, oh! Please be careful! You don't even have your pistol with you."

"I'm aware of that. And, yes, I am definitely on my guard. You don't have to worry. Where are you, by the way?"

"I'm in Interlaken and plan to go to Grindelwald tomorrow, and on Wednesday I'll head back to Zurich."

"Enjoy your last few days in Switzerland."

"I'd like to wish you the same, but all I can think to say is, be extremely careful, Regula!"

Chapter 63

Early Tuesday morning I was pondering a plan of action. I jumped when I heard someone at my door.

"Who's there?" I shouted.

"It's Karl. I need to talk to you."

"Come in."

He seemed unaware that I was in my robe and headed straight for the other chair and plopped down, facing me across the small table. The young man appeared a nervous wreck. I glanced at his face and saw fear written all over it.

He blurted, "I'm in trouble! You've got to help me."

"What kind of trouble?"

"Knupp thinks I did the killings."

"And why is that?"

"When he questioned me yesterday, it was obvious he didn't believe a word I said."

"About what?"

"He didn't buy my explanation of getting to the church late because I'd overslept. I'm also sure he didn't believe the reason I gave for driving there alone." And he added, "I wonder who told him that I got there late?"

"I can enlighten you about that. Herr Knupp attended the funeral himself."

"Really?" Then he went on, "I know he's going to pin the crimes on me, and I'm scared. I haven't slept a wink all night. I swear to God, I didn't do it!"

I said, "Okay, Karl. First you need to calm down. Then tell me your movements on Saturday morning in detail. I need to hear the truth, or I won't be able to help you."

He nodded and then began his story, "The night before the funeral, Erika told us that we should all ride to the service together as a family in Alex's SUV. Norbert said he needed to take his own car since he'd pick his boyfriend up at the train station. And I told Sis, 'no thanks, I'd rather drive myself.' Sis was clearly not pleased. I think she thought it was important to show a united front. Anyhow, she was the only one who ended up riding with Alex and his family."

I asked, "What was your reason for not joining them?"

"You want the truth, so I'll tell you. I wasn't particularly thrilled to be cooped up in a car to Davos and back with a potential murderer."

"I see." And I inquired, "Is that the reason you gave Mr. Knupp and he didn't believe you?"

He shook his head. "I told him that I get nervous riding with Alex because he's such a damned slow driver."

Chuckling, I said, "Coming from you, that sounds plausible, but then Mr. Knupp never had the pleasure of accepting a ride from you!"

Then I got serious again and said, "Please go on."

He continued, "When I got to the old stables, I saw that Norbert and Alex's cars were gone, but the little Toyota was still parked. Earlier I stood on my terrace and spotted Miss Thompson driving to the garage. I wondered why she'd come to the house before the funeral. Anyhow, when I saw her car still parked, I decided to offer her a ride down and get a chance at feeling her out. Then - -"

"What do you mean by, 'feeling her out'?" I interjected.

"You know, see if she'd be approachable in a romantic way."

"Amazing what went on in your mind on the day of your father's funeral," I remarked.

"You wanted the truth."

Then I asked, "So you had no problem riding in the same car with that particular murder suspect?"

He looked at me, dumbfounded, and exclaimed, "What? You mean she was under suspicion?"

"That never occurred to you?"

"No, and since she got killed too, I was obviously correct in not suspecting her."

"At what time did you get to the garage?"

"I didn't look at my watch, but I'd checked before I left my room. It was already five minutes past the hour then. So I quickly ran a comb through my hair, adjusted my tie, grabbed my jacket and then walked to the stables. It must have been near 10:10 when I got to my car."

He went on, "Anyway, I drove away from the garage and parked in front of the house. I had locked up before I'd walked to the stables, so I had to use the key to get back in. At the time I thought I was lucky Sis had given me Papa's key to use for the rest of my stay. Now I wish I didn't have that key. When I got to the entrance-hall, I called out, 'Miss Thompson! Are you still here? It's getting late!' I didn't get a response. I figured she might be in that room where she'd usually worked, so I went there to check.

He paused before he continued, "I first knocked and then opened the door. She was sitting there on the floor with a bag over her head. Her face was all blue. It was the most horrendous sight I'd ever seen. I ran out of the room and closed the door."

He looked straight into my eyes and went on, "My first impulse was to call the police. I'd already taken the phone out of my pocket. Then I started to think. I was the only person left in the house besides the dead girl. If I'd call the police they'd suspect me as the killer. I was scared to death and panicked. I just wanted to get the hell out of there. By the time I started the motor it was 10:16 already, so I raced down the hill."

He came to a halt. His eyes focused urgently on me, and again I was aware that this normally charming and flippant young man was in a state of fear and turmoil.

I asked, "Did you touch anything in the dictating room?"

"Of course not. I didn't go near her either. I hadn't stepped into the room farther than two meters, but even from that distance I could see she was dead and way past help. I wasn't keen on getting any closer. I felt like vomiting as it was."

Then he stared at me with his penetrating brown eyes and pleaded, "Fix it for me, please, Mrs. Huber!"

"I'm not a magician." Then I said, "I'm sure you know what you have to do."

"You want me to call Knupp and tell him the truth."

I nodded.

"He'll arrest me for sure. I mean, it looks bad for me since I lied during his questioning."

"According to you, he suspects you already. So if you're innocent, you've got nothing to lose."

He declared, "I am innocent!"

"Then the sooner you make that call, the better for you."

I walked over to the nightstand and picked up the cell phone. Handing it to him, I explained, "The number is programmed in. Scroll the menu to Ernst Knupp, and then press the call button."

That said, I headed out to the terrace to give him privacy.

Chapter 64

By the time I had finally showered and gotten myself organized, it was 10:45. When I ventured into the kitchen Helga was clearing the breakfast foods away. There was still coffee in the pot, so I poured myself a cup and sat down at the counter.

She looked at me with surprise and said, "You haven't eaten yet?"

"No. I guess I dawdled this morning," I admitted.

As she went to the refrigerator and started to take items out again, I protested, "Please, don't! I'll help myself."

"Let me cut some fruit for you, then." And before I could stop her, she sliced cantaloupe for me.

She lingered in the kitchen, and when I was done eating I said, "I've got to talk to you."

"Go ahead."

"Not here. Do you have time to go for a stroll?"

Astonished, she asked, "You want to take a walk with me?"

"Yes. I don't want to risk being overheard. Besides, a walk might do you good."

"Where are we going?"

"Oh, maybe to the creek and back."

"All right, if you want. I'm not busy at the moment. Let me put on some walking shoes. Be right back."

Rex was sitting on the lawn near the veranda, and when we reached him, I stopped and said, "Want to come with us, Rex?"

He growled.

"You don't have to," I assured him, and we walked on.

Helga commented, "The poor animal hasn't been himself lately, and who could blame him?"

We were treading by the old stables when I asked, "Have you made any plans for what to do next?"

"Plans?"

"I mean whether or not to stay at Talblick."

She replied, "I haven't given it much thought yet. It won't be easy to stay without having Mr. Sonderegger to take care of, but if Erika wants me here, I won't abandon her."

Halfway along the pasture I turned my head and noticed that Rex was slowly following us at a distance. So you've changed your mind, I thought. Good dog!

"You loved him, didn't you?"

She gazed vacantly into space, and after a long pause admitted, "You figured that out. Yes, I loved him for over forty years." Then she said briskly, "Now get to the point, Regula. You obviously have questions concerning your murder investigation. My love life is irrelevant."

"On the contrary," I stated, "Otto Sonderegger's murder was a crime of passion."

"What do you mean by that?"

"I'm sure you know."

She fixed her eyes on me, seemingly uncomprehending, and said, "I've no idea what you're implying."

"Let's stop the charade, Helga. I know it all!"

"You do?"

"You've been clever, but you gave yourself away with little statements here and there. So I've figured it all out."

"Are you accusing me of the murders?"

"Indeed, I am."

She said confidently, "I'd like to see you prove it!"

"The memoirs will be evidence, for one thing," I retorted.

"I'm not worried about the memoirs. I" - - she caught herself just in time and continued - - "mean what could possibly be in the memoirs to incriminate me?"

"Deleting the last few chapters from the document in Laura's laptop wasn't enough to keep you safe. Just because you didn't find it doesn't mean a backup disc is nonexistent!"

She just stared, and I realized she hadn't had the cognizance to delete the chapters.

I said, "You don't know much about computers, do you?"

She didn't answer, but I could tell she was starting to get unsure of herself, and I continued, "And, of course, your son's chin gave the show away."

"What on earth are you talking about?"

"When I saw you at the *Chilbi* in the company of a man in his early forties, I thought that man looked familiar. Later, when I put two and two together, I realized that I'd seen the spitting image of Otto Sonderegger in him."

She sneered, "So what if Otto and I had a son? That certainly doesn't make me a murderess!"

"True, but I'm just getting at the motive," I countered. And not giving her time to protest, I went on, "Your son spent the night at Talblick from Sunday to Monday, didn't he? It was you and your son that quarreled with Otto Sonderegger in his office early Monday morning."

"You can't prove that."

"You forget that Rita Schmied overheard part of the heated discussion. She heard Mr. Sonderegger say, 'You went behind my back and deceived me.' She was under the impression that it was a woman's voice that answered him at length. Then she heard her employer say, 'You have no legal right whatsoever.' Shortly afterwards, Mrs. Schmied saw a stranger walking down the corridor toward the entrance-hall."

She objected, "I already told you she made the whole thing up."

"The stranger was also spotted on the road on his way down from Talblick by another witness," I shot back.

She kept silent.

I stood still and looked straight at her. Her face was expressionless, but I could sense fear radiating from her body.

We continued our stroll, and I went on, "As I mentioned, you gave yourself away with several little remarks you'd made in conversation, but I won't go into all that now. You were clever when you quickly thought out a plan for how to silence Laura Thompson. However, you made one major mistake."

"And what was that?" she asked sarcastically.

"You should never have told me you still needed to change when you talked to me in the kitchen. I could see the black dress you already wore peeking out from underneath your apron. I wouldn't have given this a second thought, but later, when I pondered over the events of that morning, I connected the dots, so to speak."

Suddenly, the dam broke and it seemed she needed to vent her pent-up emotions. Her words came out in rapid succession as she exploded, "You don't understand! I loved Otto all my life, ever since I was in my twenties, only to be betrayed by him in the end. Yes, he got me pregnant when he was married to his first wife. He ordered me to give the child up for adoption, which at the time I thought was the right thing to do. Afterwards, when his wife died I was hoping he'd marry me. Instead, he married his second wife two years later.

"Then, when that selfish woman just up and left him, I thought I might have another chance. I was in my mid-forties then and not bad looking. After all, he was around sixty at that time. He occasionally made love to me, but never suggested marriage. As we got older, our relationship was more like that of good friends, or at least that's what I thought. Now I know he considered me his servant and nothing more."

She took time out to breathe and then continued in the same rapid speech, "A few years ago when it became apparent that his grandson, just like his sons, was also a disappointment to him, I had an idea. I decided to search for my son. I contacted the adoption agency but then never heard from them. So when my son, Max, got in touch with me about two weeks ago, I was overjoyed. The people from the adoption agency had contacted him, but he wasn't sure he wanted to meet me until just recently. Since I'd never gotten any news from them, I thought that my son must live abroad. To my great surprise, it turns out that he actually lives in Chur. So we decided to meet at the *Chilbi* on that Saturday."

She went on, "Then on Sunday evening we went to see a movie in Davos. Afterwards, we sat in a café and talked for hours. We had lots to catch up on. He'd been married for a short time, but the marriage ended in divorce. His adoptive parents both passed away. He'd also had some bad luck and lost his job. He was alone in the world. What a blessing that we'd found each other! When we got outside it was pouring, so I told him not to bother driving back to Chur in the rain and invited him to spend the night at Talblick instead. I also told him that the next morning I'd introduce him to someone special. I hadn't let him know who his father was. I wanted to surprise the two men facing each other and grasp how much they looked alike."

She rattled on, "So the next morning when we went to talk to Otto in his office, I was anticipating a wonderful reunion between father and son. Instead, he treated us like dirt. He said, 'Oh, it's you Helga. What do you want?' Then looking at Max he asked, 'And who is this?' Since he didn't seem to make the connection, I helped him along by saying, 'Look at him! Can't you guess?' He snapped, 'Don't play games with me. I don't know this man. Who is he and what does he want?' So I explained how we'd found each other and how he would get to know his son as well."

She took a deep breath before she continued, "He yelled at me and said that this was no son of his and how dare I go behind his back looking for him, et cetera. He went on and on about deception on my part and that this man had no legal claim to any of his money. He shook a finger at Max and told him not to expect a single penny. I was in total shock! I tried to explain to Otto that it had nothing to do with money but was a simple family matter. This apparently made him even angrier. He told us both to get out of his office. Max was obviously terrified and left immediately.

"I stayed a couple of minutes longer, trying to talk sense into Otto, but it was useless. I finally came to the realization that as far as the old man was concerned, our son was just a bastard. So I left his office in a fury, banging the door behind me. Then I wanted to give Max a ride to Davos but couldn't find him anywhere in the house. It had stopped raining for a while, and I thought he might have taken off on foot. I went outside to the front of the mansion, and sure enough, when I stood at the balustrade looking down, I saw him taking the shortcut. He called me later and said that he had wanted to get away from Talblick as fast as possible and had caught the train out of Dörfli to Davos, where his car was parked."

We had come to the part in the trail where it led uphill, and although Helga slowed down her pace, she continued her story in the same rapid fashion, panting slightly.

"Shortly after 12:00 I was descending the stairs when I heard the front door bang close. I wondered who'd left the house in the pouring rain. When I peeked outside, I was surprised to see Mr. Moritz getting into his car. I had just let him in a few minutes earlier. He was struggling with getting his umbrella closed. As he shut the car door, I noticed he'd dropped his cane. I called and waved to him, but he didn't hear me and took off. Then I got my own umbrella and went out to retrieve the cane. I stuck it into the umbrella stand in the entrance-hall with the intention of giving it back to Mr. Moritz next time he'd come by.

"I had noticed earlier that a light bulb had gone out in the dining room, so I went to exchange it. I knew some of the family was having lunch in the kitchen and in order not to disturb them; I went around the other way. From the dining room I overheard Norbert's remark about drowning the tyrant in the miniature lake. When I passed by the entrance-hall later in the afternoon and my eyes rested on Mr. Moritz's cane, I started to form my plan.

"When the time was right, I proceeded with that plan. I made sure all the household members were busy elsewhere and accounted for. I equipped myself with rubber gloves, grabbed the cane and marched down the corridor to the train room. Rex was sitting in front of the door. That dog never liked me, but when I ordered him to move aside and let me in, he obeyed. Once inside, I decided to give Otto one last chance.

"I kept my hands behind my back to hide the cane. I was pleading with him and trying to make him see things my way, but it was no use. He was preoccupied with something near the miniature lake. He totally ignored me, never even bothering to either look at me or answer. As I talked to him, he made a gesture like shooing a persistent fly out of the way. Then he muttered to himself, 'Yes, it's all running like clockwork,' all the while keeping his eyes focused on his toys. And then he turned to me and ordered, 'I'm giving it a trial run. It's perfect. Go tell everyone my project is finished and I'm ready to show it off!' Then he faced back the other way and concentrated on his silly train world again."

She went on, "An uncontrollable rage came over me. He hadn't listened to a word I'd said. I meant absolutely nothing to this man! I raised the cane and struck him down from the back using all the force I could muster. He slumped forward and his arm and shoulder crashed into the new section of his precious toy land. Then all I had to do was push his head into the lake.

"At that moment there was a tremendous clap of thunder. I quickly shoved the cane behind the curtains, took off the gloves, stuck them into my pocket, and went out the door. As I passed Rex, there was another blast of thunder, and I said, '*Platz*, Rex.' Later, I got a chance to get the cane when everyone else had left the room and passed me in the hallway, obviously thinking I went to see what had happened. I attempted to get the cane from behind the curtains, but Rex was there, guarding Otto. He growled at me furiously and bared his teeth, which made me hesitate for a second, but I managed to retrieve it. Then I hurried down the stairs at the end of the corridor and went through the garage to the outdoors, where I hid the cane in a bush nearby. I presumed the police wouldn't search the grounds in the rain, and I was correct about that. They searched the house the same day but left the outdoors for Tuesday when the thunderstorm was over."

I said, "The storm apparently was your ally in more than one way!"

She gave me an evil grin and said, "Yes, the weather was lucky for me." She continued, "Early on Tuesday morning before anyone else was up and before the police came back, I drove down to Mr. Moritz's house and threw the cane into his yard."

She came to a halt in her confession, and I said, "Then on the morning of the funeral you overheard me talking to Laura about the memoirs, and you decided to silence her. You surely came up with a plan of action quickly!"

She nodded. "I walked down the hall and heard you say that the police would want the memoirs as evidence. Until that moment, it hadn't occurred to me that Otto might have mentioned our child and the adoption in his memoirs. As soon as I overheard that, I also knew that I couldn't just destroy the incriminating chapters of the manuscript but that Laura Thompson herself would know about it and needed to be stopped. I couldn't wait until after the funeral. The police might come to take the memoirs away at any moment, or maybe Thompson would leave with them. I didn't have much time to think up a plan. I had to act fast. Some of it I left to chance."

She started to enjoy herself in showing me how clever she was as she went on, "I was already dressed for the funeral, except I had slippers on. I went to the utility room and took a big apron out of the broom closet and put it on. Then I waited in the kitchen for you. Needless to say, I had already finished taking out the platters and things for the luncheon. When you passed by, I offered you a ride to the funeral and pretended to be busy in the kitchen and still needed to change. Now I realize, I shouldn't have mentioned that. As soon as you went upstairs, I got busy.

"I grabbed a plastic shopping bag and a pair of rubber gloves from the utility room. When I got to Laura Thompson, she was bending over the bottom drawer of the desk. I don't think she heard me come in. I noticed the folded tripod leaning against the wall and felt that luck was again with me. I quickly grabbed it and struck her on the back of the head. She let out a little cry and then slumped forward, with her head landing halfway in the drawer. I first hurried to the door and shut it. Then I pulled her backward and propped her against the tripod that I'd dropped to the floor. She was clearly unconscious and I did what I had to do with the bag. That done, I looked at my watch. It wasn't even 9:30 yet, so I had more than 15 minutes until you expected me at your door.

"I found the manuscript pages sitting on the shelf. Obviously, I couldn't take away the entire memoirs. Luckily, the last chapter told about the times just before the first Mrs. Sonderegger's death, so I knew I didn't have to search far. I found the crucial chapter about my being pregnant and just grabbed that, as well as the following chapters. Before I left the room, I glanced over at Laura to make sure she wasn't stirring. Then I ran to Sonderegger's office and fed the pages into the shredder. I put the rubber gloves back in the broom closet and went upstairs to take off my apron and change into pumps."

We had arrived by the creek, where she stood still and remarked, "I have no regrets about Otto. Contrary to what he said, it was he that deceived me all my life. I didn't like what I had to do to the Thompson girl, but she knew too much."

During our entire walk I kept on guard. When we first started off, I made sure she couldn't have hidden a weapon on her person. She was wearing a pair of fitted pants with the blouse tucked in. Anything larger than a tiny pocketknife would have made a bulge. I also kept her in my vision at all times, making certain she never walked behind me. I had watched her movements, especially her hands, assuring myself she wouldn't pick up a stick or the like. But I was totally unprepared for what came next.

In a gentle voice, like the tone one would use to explain something to a child, she said, "I wish Erika wouldn't have called you back. You understand, Regula, that I can't let you escape now that you know so much. Another drowning is necessary." And with a swift movement she stooped down.

She was left-handed and I'd kept an alert eye out for any movement with that hand. I saw her pick up a good-sized rock, which I easily avoided as she hurled it at me. What I had not noticed until it was too late was the other stone she apparently had grabbed simultaneously with her right hand. She threw the two rocks in rapid succession, and when I tried to dodge the second one, it grazed my temple, catching me slightly off balance. Helga saw her advantage and jumped me like a wildcat, flinging me to the ground. We fought like boys in a schoolyard brawl, rolling around in the dirt, the difference being that I was fighting for my life. I was amazed at the woman's physical strength. She was about my height and maybe 15 pounds heavier and ten years older. The age factor didn't seem to faze her. She was clearly powerful. The woman appeared to have the strength of the insane.

We had switched positions a couple of times and I was suddenly aware that we were getting nearer to the creek. When she had managed to get back on top again, she maneuvered my head dangerously close to the water. At one point I was able to move my knee upward from under her and jammed it hard into her ribs. She cried out in pain, but then her hands were around my throat.

Her face was only a few inches away from mine, and I saw determination in her eyes as she tightened her grip. I fought a good fight, trying with all my might to pull her hands away, but she was stronger, and I felt myself weakening. I closed my eyes, hoping she'd think it was all over. The pressure on my throat increased and I had trouble breathing. I kept my eyes shut and told myself, just keep pretending and don't panic!

Suddenly, I heard a bark, then a growl, and in another split second her grip on my throat relaxed. I opened my eyes and saw terror in Helga's. Then I glanced beyond her face. Rex was holding the housekeeper's neck between his jaws. I took in a few deep breaths and then wriggled myself out from underneath her. I sat on the ground for a moment, rubbing my sore neck. Then I got to my feet. This experience has been way too close for comfort! I thought.

I looked at Rex, his fangs still holding on to her throat and realized that I had to be singularly careful of what I would say to him. I had no idea about the command language in dog training, particularly not in Swiss-German. I wanted him to guard her, of course, but if I uttered the wrong command, he might go for the kill.

So I settled on, "*Platz*, Rex!"

He slowly let go of her neck and then sat down next to her.

I exclaimed, "Good boy!" and bent down to pet him, thankful that this amazing dog had saved my life.

In the meantime Helga had recuperated from the shock and started to get up, but immediately Rex snarled and bared his fangs, and she lay down again.

I reached into my trousers' pocket, grabbed the phone, scrolled the menu to Ernst Knupp, and pressed the call button.

Chapter 65

As the plane took off from Zurich, I glanced out of the window and surveyed the city from above. When the aircraft gained in altitude, the buildings below appeared smaller and smaller. Soon my native town disappeared from view altogether and was replaced with fields, farmland and forest.

I looked over at Peter and said, "I'm sorry our trip didn't go exactly according to plan."

"Now that's an understatement! Next time we go on vacation, I'll keep you on a leash!" Then he became grave and, glancing at the bruises on my neck, said, "I'm just relieved that I've got you back and that you are okay."

"Me too!"

A bit later he asked, "How did you get wise to Helga? Was she one of your prime suspects all along?"

I replied, "Like always, at the beginning of an investigation, I suspect everyone. This case was no exception. Actually, it was you who finally steered me in the right direction."

"What did I do to deserve such credit?"

"Remember when we talked Friday evening before the funeral?"

"Sure, but what did I say that was so revealing to you?"

I smiled and said, "You pointed out that there were basically three main motives for murder: greed, passion and self-preservation."

Surprised, he remarked, "Didn't you know that already? I was just trying to be a wise guy."

"Yes, of course, but it made me look at the suspects from a different perspective. Up until then, I sort of was stuck in the 'greed' mode."

"Okay, but how did that get you to the housekeeper?"

"I saw Otto Sonderegger's grandson for the first time attending the funeral and he resembled his grandfather a great deal. Then I came to realize I'd recently seen someone else this young man looked like. Later, when I stood close to the grandson at the luncheon, I remembered that he resembled the man whom I'd seen Helga with at the carnival. At the time I was getting uneasy about not being able to find Laura among the guests and didn't dwell on it.

"Then on Sunday and Monday I sat in my room for hours mulling over what each person had told me from day one. I had briefly done this once before without much result. Finally, I went from the point of view of considering the murder as a crime of passion. Little by little, I came to the conclusion that most of the information I'd gathered pointed to Helga."

"How so?"

"Erika told me she always suspected the housekeeper was in love with her father. Then when I talked to Helga one day, she informed me that she'd been absent from Talblick for several months at one time. She explained it away as having had to take care of her mother recovering from surgery. Lotti overheard a fraction of her grandfather's dictation about some adoption. Then after Otto Sonderegger's murder I learned from the cleaning woman about the quarrel she'd overheard. She first thought she had heard a woman's voice talking with Sonderegger in his office. Then, when seeing the stranger leave, she was confused and figured the person she'd heard talking to her employer must have been a man after all."

I continued, "Fritz Moritz said that Hans Weber mumbled something about someone else washing sheets in the laundry room. And then, as I said, I remembered the man at the carnival and felt sure that must have been Helga's son. When I went to see Laura Thompson in Davos, she said her boss wanted to add some event from the present to his memoirs, which I felt certain had to do with the encounter he'd had that morning in his office. Then there were several remarks Helga made after Sonderegger was killed that gave her away. For example - -"

Peter interjected, "Before you go on, clarify a couple of things for me."

"What things?"

"I take it that you figured Helga's absence from Talblick was during the latter part of her pregnancy and that she went somewhere else to have the baby?"

"Of course."

"What you told me makes sense, except what the masseur guy said about someone washing sheets. Explain that."

"All right. I had already deduced that there had been two people in the office with Sonderegger, namely Helga and her son. But I couldn't understand how the son got there since he apparently had left on foot. I doubted that he'd hiked up on such a stormy day. So when Mr. Moritz remarked that the masseur muttered something about a load of sheets someone was washing, I said to myself, *what sheets*? The most likely person to be using the washing machine besides Hans Weber would be Helga. Aha, I thought, she had told me she'd gone to see a movie the night before. She might have done so together with her son, then invited him to spend the night, and these were his sheets she'd washed."

Peter said, "I understand now. So keep going."

"Where did I leave off?"

"You were going to tell me about Helga's self-incriminating remarks."

"Oh, yeah. When I asked her how she felt about Otto Sonderegger's will, she answered, 'Blood is thicker than water.' She said this showing extreme emotion. At the time I thought she must feel strongly for Alex, Norbert and Karl. Then later, I realized she'd been thinking about her own son when saying those words. Also, when Helga stated so vehemently that Mrs. Schmied must have made the whole thing up, meaning the stranger as well as overhearing a quarrel, she achieved just the opposite. I felt convinced there had in fact been a man unknown to the cleaning woman in the house and that she'd overheard the dispute.

"One of the biggest mistakes she made was telling me that when she'd first heard of the tragic news about Otto Sonderegger, she had dropped the vase with the flowers."

He protested, "Now, Regula! You've got to admit that dropping the vase full of water was extremely clever of her. She covered herself in case anyone would notice she got wet when drowning the old man."

"That was too clever for her own good," I replied.

"Come again?"

"Don't forget, I know Helga well. Not only from my present visit, but I'd known her for years when I was a child and teenager. This woman is competence personified. If anyone else would have let go of a vase under stress, I could have understood, but I found it hard to believe of Helga. And if the mishap really had occurred, she would have been too proud to point out that fact to me."

"Yes, I see your reasoning now," he said.

"On the other hand, offering me a ride to the funeral was smart of her and not overdone."

"What do you mean?"

I explained, "At the time I had the feeling that Helga offered me the ride on the spur of the moment out of consideration for me. It made sense that we should arrive at the church before the family. Later, I realized that she picked me as her alibi, so to speak."

"I'm not sure I follow you."

"Remember, at the time I thought she still needed to take care of things in the kitchen and then go up and change. She knew that she only had about twenty minutes or so to commit the crime and get rid of the manuscript pages. She figured I'd also be her alibi when the two of us would be arriving back at Talblick after the funeral."

"Except that you noticed she was already completely dressed below her apron."

"Actually, that didn't register with me until later when I'd already suspected Helga. I might have easily overlooked the black dress."

Then he asked, "With whom had you originally planned to drive to the funeral?"

"We hadn't discussed it, but I'd assumed Erika would give me a ride. I didn't know that she was going with Alex. So before I went to change, I quickly stopped at Erika's door and told her I was riding with Helga.

"Overall the two murders, although simple, were cleverly thought out and executed. Helga has a quick mind."

Peter remarked, "Hard to believe that it took such a smart woman over forty years to figure out that Otto Sonderegger didn't return her feelings!"

"How does the saying go? 'Love is Blind'?"

"Must be so."

After a pause he said, "Rex seems an amazing dog."

"You can say that again! That phenomenal four-legged friend saved my life."

"Do you think he knew that Helga was the killer?"

"I don't believe we can credit the canine with that kind of intellect. His dislike of her was triggered by instinct." And I added, "When he growled at my order to come along on the walk, I knew his animosity was geared toward Helga and not me. At the same time I sensed the anxiety in Helga. I felt positive that she was terrified of the dog."

Then I said, "I feel awful about Laura. Did I tell you she was supposed to be on this plane with us?"

He shook his head.

I fell silent, and Peter took my hand in his. We didn't mention the murder case anymore for the rest of our flight home.

EPILOGUE

One day in January of the next year I was sitting at the desk in my Pasadena office working on a new case. The task was tedious, and I decided to take a break from the brainwork and check my e-mail messages.

There was one from Erika, and it read:

"Dear Regula,

"I hope you had a Merry Christmas. I didn't send out cards, so I belatedly wish you and Peter the best in the New Year.

"I meant to write sooner, but kept putting it off. *Mea culpa!*

"We have tons of snow at the moment and the skiing is great, but every time I ski *Parsenn*, I think of Papa, as it was his favorite.

"Helga was convicted and will spend the rest of her life in prison. You might be interested to know the contents of Papa's will. He actually did make an addition to his will about two weeks before he died, but he didn't cut anyone off. He left Helga, Mr. Moritz and Laura Thompson each a legacy of a substantial amount. As in his previous will, the rest of the fortune is equally divided between Alex, Norbert, Karl and me. I also inherited Talblick, as I knew I would.

"I don't know what happens to Helga's portion yet, but we'll make certain that she will not get a single penny. Laura's share goes to her parents, which doesn't make their suffering any easier, I'm sure.

"I guess the boys and I are millionaires, but what does that really mean? With big money, bigger responsibilities and headaches follow, I presume.

"To my great surprise, the boys have visited frequently in the last few months. Almost every weekend, one or another of them shows up. They all seem drawn to Papa's grave. I visit there often myself. Right now the grave is covered with snow, and yesterday I noticed someone had placed a pair of miniature skis next to the gravestone. Little trinkets have been put there all along. Among them are a king from a chess set, playing cards, a horse, a building that resembled the Sondereggli, a train, and now the skis. Most of these mini-objects are made from wood, and I suspect Mr. Moritz is their creator.

"As for Talblick, I don't know yet what I'll do with the place. The mansion was way too big for the three of us already, and now that I'm by myself its size is totally out of proportion. I might sell it or rent it out, and if I decide to keep the house, I certainly won't live in it. I might have it converted into a hotel. Wouldn't that make Papa happy, if he's watching, that is!

"I have sad news about Rex. The poor dog missed Papa so much that he starved himself. In the end he was so weak that I had to have him put to sleep.

"Hope everything is well with you.

"Warmest regards,

Erika

PS: You were right about Claude. I caught him in bed with his receptionist."

That evening, I stepped out on the back porch of our home in Merida and looked up at the full moon. I imagined the lonesome autocrat surveying his gravesite from above, chuckling,

"Hard to fathom: I have a devoted family after all!"

www.ingramcontent.com/pod-product-compliance
Lightning Source LLC
Chambersburg PA
CBHW020558260626
47157CB00003B/756